The Triumph

AND OTHER STORIES

by

HENRY ZVI UCKO

For John, who listened and liked, and the only colleague who ever embraced me, affectionately, Henry Zvi.

The Sverdlik Press
Durham, NC

The Sverdlik Press
P.O. Box 52084
Durham, NC 27717

Copyright ©1993 by Henry Zvi Ucko
Library of Congress Catalog Card No. 93-092736

ISBN No. 0-9637399-0-5

TABLE OF CONTENTS

INTRODUCTION

Many of the biographies of famous violinists or pianists begin with the statement that the artists made their debut at the tender age of five or six. My literary career began somewhat later, in my early teens, with a highly nationalistic poem in support of German schools in post World War I Baltic states. Unfortunately – or maybe fortunately – the opus which appeared in a publication of the "Gymnasium" I attended in my native city of Koenigsberg, Germany, is lost, an interesting testament to the feeling of a completely assimilated German-Jewish boy. Another early attempt that was published in the *Koenigsberger Hartungsche Zeitung*, the renowned liberal newspaper of my hometown, is also lost. I regret that because "Tante Strom" was a lovely vignette, the portrait of a nature- and children-loving elderly lady.

Book reviews, features, program notes, radio talks, story manuscripts and clippings, all went to the bottom of the sea when, on my escape from Nazi Germany, the boat I was traveling on was sunk in the English Channel on its way to Central America.

But unbeknown to me, two stories had survived. On a hint from Dr. Amy Grant, a former Religious School student of mine, my wife, Lenora, searched the yellowed back issues of the *Berlin Israelitisches Familienblatt* in the archives of the Leo Baeck Institute in New York. There they were – "Teshuvah (Return)" [1937]; and "Gevatter Tod (Godfather Death)" [1936]. I translated both into English and they are found in the second part of this volume.

All the other stories were written more recently in English in this country. My family and friends have kept urging me to put them into print. I resisted a good while. But in the meantime I tested them, reading them to listeners of different ages, nationalities and occupations. Since my audience seemed to enjoy them—very few fell asleep—I have finally decided to have the stories published, hopefully also for your enjoyment.

H. Z. U.

PART I

THE TRIUMPH

We boys called her the "Steamroller." My mother said that was not nice and forbade us to do it. My father of course agreed with mother but could not help grinning when he heard it. He had a sense of humor. Mother had not.

The fact is that Aunt Estella had several chins and seemed in need of using her arms like oars to propel herself forward. She was one massive bulk of fat and had an ugly wart on her cheek. Besides, she had the habit of criticizing everything and everybody, except her brilliant son, the Doctor. No wonder that whenever she appeared as a visitor, we tried to stay out of sight in the Children's Room.

She had one redeeming feature though. She could do card tricks. She did not do them often, but when she did I turned up to watch her. You had to hand it to her. She was pretty good at it. Especially when she made a card disappear from the deck and let you find it under the table.

I would have given my best marble – the big transparent one with the ivory bird in it – to find out how she did it. My father could do a few simple tricks too, but he always showed us afterwards how it was done. But not she. Not a hint. She just sat there with a stony face, the black hat with the wide brim on her head (she never took it off), only cracking a small satisfied smile when she saw wonder and astonishment written on our faces.

I would beg, "Aunt Estella, how do you do it? Please Aunt, show me how to do it." But it was like talking to the Shakespeare monument in the park. You could not move her.

"Magicians do not reveal their secrets," she said. And that was all.

Once I tried to trap her by crawling under the table, but she became rather unpleasant and I was ordered out of the room. I did not think that was fair and harbored thoughts of revenge.

It would not be easy, and I had no allies. Because my older brother managed to get along well with even the most disagreeable uncles and aunts. You could not count on my father; he was mostly at the Club. And my mother? She would not have dared to stand up to Aunt Estella at all although she had good reason to be annoyed with her.

This was why: The Steamroller was considered an intellectual authority. And so my mother, with understandable pride, had shown her the report card of my brother, who was an excellent student. She could have saved herself the trouble. Instead of bestowing the expected praise, Aunt Estella had put the card aside, hardly looking at it, and had launched into a lengthy account of the honors and awards that her Freddie, the Doctor, had received and continued to collect.

I felt sorry for my mother's disappointment, and was angry that she valued Aunt Estella's judgment so exceedingly. So I waited for an opportunity to show the Steamroller that her judgment was not infallible.

My opening came when my brother wanted to show off a bit before the aunt. We had a children's marionette theater which had a set amount of puppets for a few plays. But we were not satisfied with a limited repertoire and had manufactured additional marionettes ourselves. My brother whom I admired greatly had done a nice job with it, and when Aunt Estella came to visit, he proudly showed her the figures he had cut out, pasted and wired. Of course, he pointed out to her that he himself had made the puppets. But although my brother was a favorite with the Steamroller and enjoyed the privilege of walking her dog and playing on her old Baldwin, he could not escape her criticism.

"Well now, Jack," she said. "I must say that is not exactly a professional job. You may have tried but you surely could have done better."

I saw my brother's face fall. He was clearly hurt.

This gave me an idea. I stole back into our playroom, picked up one of our best factory-made puppets and presented it to the Steamroller for inspection.

"Look Aunt," I said with leering humility. "This one I made. What do you think of it?"

She took one condescending look at it and then with some unwilling grace pronounced the following judgment.

"Considering your age, one might call it almost acceptable." That was all I had been waiting for.

"For your information, Aunt Estella," I said triumphantly and as formally as I knew to put it, "this puppet was not made by me, but is the finished product of a factory. See how you fell into my trap. He, he, he!"

I do not know if, at that age, I knew what sarcastic meant, but I did laugh sarcastically. And jumping around and highly pleased with myself, I repeated, "He, he! You fell into my trap. He, he!"

The effect was dramatic. For once my brother looked admiringly at me. My mother was speechless, and trembling awaited the aunt's reaction. It came fast.

The Steamroller got red in the face. Closing the open pocketbook with a sharp snap, she got up, started remonstrating loudly,

"I never . . . " but did not finish and rowed out of the room as fast as she could, her arms working wildly.

When my father came home from the Club, he was informed of the incident. I watched him with great apprehension. He had a temper and things could become dangerous.

At first, he seemed to consider the matter from the humorous side and I started breathing easier. But when he heard of my triumphal dance, and especially of the repeated "He, he, he's," the tempest broke loose. He grabbed me and I got a licking with the walking cane that unfortunately was still in his hand. In addition, he ordered, "No supper tonight!"

Tearless and with terrible thoughts of vengeance against the Steamroller, I withdrew into the Children's Room.

Night had fallen and I stood in the dark, unrepentant, murder in my heart. Later my mother came and stealthily brought me something to eat. Bless her heart—maybe she was on my side. Watching my brother slighted again must have been too much even for her long-suffering soul.

First I did not touch anything. One had his pride. But after a while, I ate. It was late and I really was very hungry.

THE DAGGER THRUST

Allan was looking forward to this family visit. That Dr. Schwartzbart, a distant cousin of his father, must be quite a guy. At the dinner table, the story was told that as a student he had fought a pistol duel, and his lower jaw had been shattered. He was a widower – at least so it seemed because there was never any mention of Mrs. Schwartzbart – and he lived with his unmarried daughter. Her name was Elvira. And she was, adding to the unusual, a professional dancer. All this excited Allan's curiosity.

After their arrival, Dr. Schwartzbart turned out to be a bit of a disappointment. True there was a scar on his chin and the whole face seemed somewhat distorted. But otherwise he was simply a short, stocky man with a good appetite. He was so friendly and good-natured that Allan began to wonder if the story of the duel was true.

But Elvira was mysterious and exciting. She was tall and slim. Her black hair fell streaming over her shoulders. She wore a bright yellow cape over her dress and shoes with extremely high heels. She immediately took possession of Allan, smoothed his hair with both hands, which made the bracelets on her wrists dangle and jingle, and told the blushing twelve-year-old that she just loved to kiss noses. She promptly indulged in her habit and Allan felt half honored, half embarrassed.

More was to come. It being a clear frosty day, she asked him if he would like to go skating. Allan said his skates were not much good.

"Nonsense," she waved away his hesitant objection. "I haven't got mine here at all. We will just rent some at the skating rink."

She was already dressed in a light blue ski suit, her face framed by a white tasseled cap.

"Where do we go?"

Allan led the way. In the most natural manner, she took his arm, and the two walked fast, their breath showing in the cold air.

"I warn you," panted Allan. "I do not know any fancy stuff. Only some plain forward racing."

"That's O.K. I will show you some figure skating."

At the rink, she rented some first rate skates for both of them. On the ice, she began to show Allan a few simple figures, but soon she left him standing by a bench and abandoned herself completely to her own enjoyment. She seemed to be as good a dancer on the ice as on the stage. In a short time a circle of onlookers had formed around her, watching her graceful movements and applauding enthusiastically after each daring jump. Suddenly she seemed to remember Allan. She looked around, raced over to him and came to a screeching stop in front of him. Flushed and radiant, she smiled at him and kissed the tip of his nose. Allan felt this was absolutely uncalled for. He took out his handkerchief and blew his nose. Noting his embarrassment, she quickly led him away.

Amendments had to be made. So in the evening while the older folks were busy looking at family photos, Elvira came quietly up behind Allan's chair. Putting her arms around his shoulders, she bent over him and whispered, "Have you ever been to the Opera?" Yes, they had sent him once to see *Hansel and Gretel* but he did not much care for it.

"But I need somebody to go with me tomorrow night to *Rigoletto*. I want you to take me."

"What happens in *Rigoletto*?"

They went into a corner of the dimly lit den. Allan settled himself in the depths of a wide armchair, and Elvira sat at his feet on the floor. Then she told him the story of the court jester whose daughter falls in love with a Duke, and is seduced and later abandoned by him.

"You know 'seduced'?" Elvira inquired.

"Sure." Allan nodded wisely.

"Well," continued Elvira, "Rigoletto, the father, swears revenge and hires a professional killer to murder the Duke. But Gilda, the daughter, decides to save her faithless lover by sacrificing her own life for his."

"How does she do that?"

"If you come with me, you will find out. It happens during a terrible storm."

She got up. "Good night, Allan."

He pulled back instinctively.

"I am not going to kiss you, stupid." And she walked over to the living room to join her father and the rest of the family.

Allan got up, murmured something in the direction of the living room and went to bed. His fantasy was stirred. That *Rigoletto* was certainly different from silly *Hansel and Gretel.* Allan was some thing of a poet himself, although nobody knew it. But his poems were mostly lyrical outpourings about nature and dying, and he abhorred violence. And there would be violence. Stabbing, strangling, shooting, who knew what. Besides there was that storm. Though he was ashamed to admit it, he was deathly afraid of thunder and lightning. He tried to console himself with the thought that these would be only stage effects, and the idea of going with Elvira pleased him greatly. He would wear his blue suit and the bowtie with the polka dots. And he would put a little perfume on his shirt and – and – and he fell asleep.

Elvira surely knew how to make an entrance. Clad in a black velvet gown slit to show her long legs, a diamond-studded silver band holding her hair, she pushed Allan in front of her along the first row and found their two seats in the center. She looked around with a satisfied smile and handed Allan the program. He savored its strong print smell and read the list of characters, trying to learn their names. Borsa. Marullo. Monterone. Sparafucile. He gave up and began to study the synopsis of the action. He had barely gotten to the second scene when the lights dimmed. The chatter and laughter of the audience died down. There was only the glow from the orchestra pit and an expectant silence. A slight gradually increasing ripple of applause was heard and suddenly to Allan's surprise the curly head of the young conductor popped up right in front of him, bowing but turning around quickly and raising the baton in the usual attention-demanding gesture.

Unfortunately Allan did not have the family flair for music and he did not understand Italian. In spite of what Elvira had told him, he could not follow the action. He often was at a loss to recognize who was who in the black capes on the dark stage. During Gilda's famous "Caro Nome" aria, he actually dozed off, and was called to order by Elvira's elbow. But during the intermission, when Elvira treated him to some exotic drink in the gorgeous foyer, he was again wide awake. When they returned to the auditorium for the last act, he looked down into the orchestra pit and saw with indignation that the tympani player was reading a newspaper that he had spread out over the kettledrums. A gray-haired lady was rehearsing a shrill figure on the piccolo over and over again. Elvira, who was leaning over the railing next to Allan, said, "She is playing the passage that indicates the lightning during the storm."

"I see." Allan got uneasy at the mention of the storm.

"Is this the act where Gilda sacrifices herself?"

"Yes, dear."

"Oh."

The curtain rose on the last act with its divided scenery-dilapidated inn of the hired assassin on one side, a sinister riverside landscape on the other. Again two black-caped persons were conversing in the dark. One, though in man's clothing, had a woman's voice. Apparently it was Gilda. Allan thought it all rather confusing. But then things got lively. The interior of the inn lit up; the Duke stormed in and delivered "La Donna E Mobile" in his ringing tenor voice. Allan applauded wildly with the rest of the audience.

But the respite was short-lived. That piccolo passage shrilled. Lightning was seen. Distant thunder was heard, and the sound of the rising wind, produced by humming human voices. It was all so natural, Allan got cold. And now the action becomes quite clear. The bravo is ready to thrust the dagger into the heart of anybody who comes to seek shelter from the storm at the inn. And there is Gilda, knocking at the door. Knocking, knocking again. Every knock is accentuated by piccolo shrill and lightning. And now the door is opened. Gilda runs in, right into the uplifted dagger. A desperate cry. The storm rages. And the orchestra whistles and crashes with deafening noise. Allan could not take it any longer—

In the darkness of his bedroom, Allan lay and stared into its shadowy corners. Images passed by. The laughing Duke. The black-bearded assassin. The shrieking Gilda. And at the end, when he had looked once more at the stage in spite of all his fright, what had he seen? And—oh God—here it seemed to come out of the

15

shadows. A sack and a dead body in it. He reached for the pocket-knife on his night table, and held it in readiness under the covers. There was a noise. Somebody opened his door.

It was Elvira. She came up to his bed. "Allan?" He gave no sign of recognition, his eyes firmly closed. She walked out pulling the door to, but not closing it entirely.

"Is he asleep?" That was Dr. Schwartzbart's voice.

"Yes."

Allan slipped down from the bed, tiptoed toward the door, but froze when they began talking again.

"What are you laughing about? What is so funny?"

"Oh, Dad, it actually is not so funny. But it was so cute. You know the last act of *Rigoletto*, when Gilda comes to save the Duke?"

"Of course, I know. So what happened?"

"Allan – he was so cute."

The boy behind the door dreaded to hear more. Trembling he pulled out the blade of the pocketknife that he still held clutched in his hand. There was no escape. He had to listen.

"Cute?" he heard Dr. Schwartzbart ask.

"Yes, at the height of the storm, when Gilda ran into the inn, he grabbed my arm. 'No, Elvira, no,' he gasped and covered his eyes with his hands. Oh, he was so cute. So cute. I could have kissed his nose right away."

Allan stood motionless. Furious. Indeed she deserved to be stabbed – that long-legged spider.

Instead, he threw the knife to the floor and himself on the bed, burying his tear-stained shame in the pillow.

IN CONSEQUENCE OF RAIN

I find it a little embarrassing to tell this story. It is definitely somewhat risqué. So if you do not care for this type of thing, just skip it. No offense meant or taken. My only excuse is that I was still very young; not a child though, but a young man, sixteen maybe, or seventeen. I do not remember exactly.

The fact is that I had become interested in a certain Mrs. Wallace. No, she was not divorced nor a widow. She was then about forty, not especially good-looking. But she had a way of walking that excited my fantasy considerably. Her husband was a muscular, rather coarse fellow. They had a son, an only child, who had trouble with his Latin. And that is how I got connected with the family, because I had taken on the job of tutoring young Wallace. Now that boy had absolutely no head for Latin, but seeing how his mother adored him, I carefully avoided critical comments on his mental capacity.

Certain days, Mrs. Wallace hcr first name was Kate – chose to come into the room where I taught the boy, and watch the progress of the lesson. Though I did not particularly care for this, it gave me a chance to talk to her, making quite a show of sharing her concern for her son's learning problem. She in turn praised my pedagogic skill and my intelligence. She had an animated way of talking and occasionally touched my arm the way some outgoing women do. I knew it was done only for emphasis, but I liked it. It seemed to establish some kind of conspiratorial familiarity between us.

At times, she would mention a show or movie that we had both seen and casually remark, again with a slight tap on my arm or shoulder, that her husband preferred wrestling. But when I thought I could deepen the conspiracy by suggesting that she did not care to attend such coarse entertainment, I was taken aback and surprised to hear her say that she always accompanied her husband and enjoyed it a lot.

Occasionally when I had to change the time for a lesson, I would call, and if by luck she answered herself, we had a short telephone conversation. Once I got daring and asked her if I could pick her up, and of course the boy too, for a visit to the zoo, but she said she was busy that afternoon.

It was a rainy day and I was coming up the little hill on Museum Lane, when I saw Kate Wallace a short distance ahead of me. I recognized her by that special way of walking that so excited my senses. She wore a flimsy black raincoat and a rather becoming cap that allowed her hair to slip out in disorderly profusion. Speeding up, I managed to overtake her and greeted her somewhat out of breath.

At that moment, the rain changed into a heavy shower and I suggested to seek shelter in the Museum. There was a little side entrance nearby, and quite a few people were running toward it. We entered and found ourselves in a small lobby packed with other fugitives from the downpour. A sign, "Use Main Entrance," and a locked inner door kept us where we were.

It was hot and damp in the overheated hall. More and more passers-by came in. There was hardly any room to move. We stood close to each other like in a crowded bus. People spoke in subdued tones as in a church or funeral parlor. It had gotten very dark outside, and there were no lights in the hall.

And then it happened. I knew I would blush and hesitate when I came to this part of the story. But I have said already that we were standing in extremely close proximity. And so it happened. Yes indeed, it happened that my hand stole into the pocket of Mrs. Wallace's raincoat, and that—you must forgive me, I was very young and full of yearning—that I began to move my fingers in a cautious caress within that pocket. At the same time, I talked businesslike to her about her son's difficulty with the conjugation of the Latin irregular verbs. She did not move away from me, and there was not the slightest change of expression in her face.

Suddenly somebody called out, "I think the rain has stopped!" Everybody started moving toward the door, and in a moment Kate and I were standing in the street. She looked impatiently at her watch. "My husband is expecting me for lunch. See you later." Quickly she boarded a bus that had stopped, and was gone.

As I stood there in utter confusion, I felt something had remained in my hand, when I withdrew it from the fatal pocket. It was a glove, one glove only. Perplexed, I stared at it and wondered if she would miss it. But she probably had many other pairs.

ALL ABOUT REVELATION

As much as I respected my father, I was never quite sure that the "true stories" he used to tell — and he had a rich repertoire of them — were one hundred percent true. But since he called the characters in the following story by name, and I knew some of them personally, I am inclined to think that it is indeed based on fact. And I shall try to relate it as much as possible in his own words. That should not be too difficult because I have heard it many times. I only regret that you cannot hear him tell the story himself because he was quite an actor and knew how to dramatize. So much for the introduction, and now listen.

David Abramovitz and Moishe Cohn — in the telephone directory he was listed as Maurice Cohen, but everybody called him Moishe Cohn — the two did not get along too well. David, a house painter by profession, was known as a practical joker, and everybody enjoyed his antics, so long as they were directed against somebody else. Moishe, who had no particular occupation except some connection with the synagogue and the burial society, walked around with a sullen face, always absorbed in fulfilling this or that ritual requirement, and resentful of those who did not feel the same need. David called Moishe a religious fanatic, and Moishe called David an unbelieving fool. Both were not entirely wrong, and so they made disparaging remarks about each other, regardless if the adversary was present or not.

David was not as irreligious as Moishe made him out to be, but some of Moishe's idiosyncrasies went on his nerves. For instance, Moishe was in the habit of remaining in the synagogue when the service was over. That seemed to provoke David.

"Why does he not leave when everybody else does? What is he doing there all by himself?" he used to ask his fellow worshippers.

"What do YOU care?" they would counter goodnaturedly. "Maybe he wants to pray some more. You know how he is!"

That answer did not satisfy David, and so one evening he went back to the synagogue after Services. Quietly he climbed the stairs to the women's balcony. Careful not to make any noise, he descended to the railing in front, went on his knees and looked down. Sure enough, there was Moishe in the dimly lit sanctuary, standing at his seat, swaying forth and back while reciting prayers in a half-loud singsong. David watched for a few minutes. He was about to turn around and steal away, when an idea—a typical David Abramovitz idea—struck him. Crouching behind the banister, he called in a soft high tremulous voice,

"Reb Moi-she, Reb Moi-oi-she."

Moishe stopped in his prayers, looked up, shook his head and continued his singsong. David tried again.

"Reb Moi-she, Reb Moi-i-she."

It really sounded eerie in the empty synagogue. Moishe was now visibly upset. He left his seat, walked up to the cantor's stand, grabbed it with both hands, bent over it and remained in a listening position.

Extremely satisfied with his success, David made another effort and managed to make it sound even more mysterious.

"Reb Moi-oi-she, Reb Moi-oi-oi-she."

And he raised his head a little over the railing to see more clearly. Moishe straightened up and stood for a moment motionless.

Suddenly he raised his head toward the Eternal Light before the Ark, spread out his arms and in an agitated voice stirred by emotion called out,

"Here I am. Speak to me! Thy servant is listening."

This was more than David had expected. He beat a quick retreat and hastened home.

When he told his wife what had happened, her reaction was different from what it used to be. Generally she responded with a hearty laugh to her husband's pranks. But when she heard that Moishe Cohn had really believed that God was calling him, she got quite serious.

"That was no joke, David. You went too far. And don't you tell anybody about this!"

David, who had not been feeling so good about the whole affair, was willing to take her advice. He kept the incident to himself. But after a while, he could not stand it any longer. It was too good a story to be kept under his hat. So the next Wednesday, when the poker club met, he told confidentially what had happened, and made quite a performance of it. The guys laughed themselves sick.

Of course, now it did not take long for the story to get around. It also reached the rabbi. Young Rabbi Solomon was not too fond of Mr. Cohen. As a matter of fact, Moishe had given him a hard time whenever the rabbi had tried to introduce some innovative changes in the Service. Although he would never call the rabbi by his first name as some of the younger group did—a practice condemned as disrespectful by Moishe—he did not hesitate to argue heatedly against any deviation from the traditional norm. Nevertheless Rabbi Solomon apparently felt that he had to do something to prevent Moishe from becoming the laughing stock of the community and to cushion his inevitable fall from heavenly illusion to down-to-earth reality.

Consequently on the next Sabbath, he took as his sermon topic the phenomenon of revelation. He pointed out that only extraordinary personalities like Moses or the prophets had been privileged to hear the voice of God, that this type of revelation was practically non-existent in our time and age. The congregants – at least those who did not habitually fall asleep during the rabbi's sermon – elbowed their neighbors, turned around, looked at each other and nodded toward Moishe Cohn's seat. He was listening attentively, ready to catch any heresy which might come from the pulpit.

After the Service, when shaking hands with the rabbi, Moishe said,

"So in your opinion, God does not speak to anybody anymore in person?"

"At least not in the literal sense of the word," the rabbi responded mildly. They got into a lengthy argument. Finally Moishe said abruptly, "I disagree," and walked off.

The matter might have ended there, had it not been for David Abramovitz's yearning for applause. He loved to have an audience, and at the slightest provocation was willing to tell his revelation story. Although by now almost everyone was familiar with it, except Moishe himself, they liked to hear it again, especially for the benefit and amusement of a newcomer to the congregation.

So one day, while they were waiting in the synagogue for the tenth man to arrive to make up the *minyan* (quorum), they urged David to reenact his prank. He was only too happy to comply, but just when he had reached the high point of the show, when to the delight of his listeners, he made the call, "Moi-oi-oi-she" ring in a greatly perfected high tremolo, an angry voice was heard.

"You bandit! You idiot! You good-for-nothing fool!"

They all turned toward the entrance. There stood Moishe,

trembling in a furious rage.

In embarrassed silence, the group stood motionless, looking from Moishe to David and from David to Moishe, waiting for further developments. They were quick to come. Moishe grabbed a heavy tome from a bookshelf, raised it with both hands high over his head, and advanced threateningly toward David, while shouts of "No, Moishe, no!" were heard. He did not get a chance to deliver the intended blow. David knocked the book out of Moishe's hands. It fell to the ground, and so did the two combatants in the ensuing wrestling and punching match. A most deplorable sight! Two grown men, not so young anymore either, rolling around on the floor of the synagogue. Of course, some able-bodied men intervened and separated the fighting parties, but what a scandal! What a scandal!

"Stop it! You should be ashamed of yourselves."

There was universal condemnation of both. And the two, with hanging heads, pressing handkerchiefs against some bleeding cuts, but still muttering threats and curses, left the sanctuary in disgrace.

A moment of uncomfortable consternation.

But then the *shammes* (sexton) was sent after them in a hurry. After all, without them there was no *minyan*. So they were brought back, put in different seats as far apart as possible, and the Service began.

TOWARD FREEDOM

It was fortunate that Leo Schmuelovitz's wife was one hundred percent Aryan (although she had formally converted to Judaism) and that her brother was a high ranking officer in the S.S. Therefore she dared to go to the Gestapo in hopes that by the brother's intervention Leo would be released from the concentration camp and be permitted to leave Germany on a visa to the Dominican Republic.

The reception in her brother's office was not too cordial.

"You shouldn't have come, Hilde. I really do not know if I can help you. In any case, you will have to see Commander Gottlieb. I can call and ask him to act favorably on your request, but the decision is entirely his. You have to excuse me now. I am very busy."

When Commander Gottlieb looked up from his desk, and saw the buxom Hilde and her tearstained face, he decided to play the jovial father part. He came out from behind his desk, put an arm around her, accidentally stroking her breast, and said jokingly,

"So you want to speed your little Jew boy out of the country. Well! Well! That comes from getting mixed up with a Semite."

"Please," pleaded Hilde, putting his arm down, "I appeal to your German conscience. Jewish or not, he is my husband. I will stay here in the Fatherland, but it is my duty to save his life."

Gottlieb would have liked to slap her face, but he was not sure of her brother's reaction in case she would tell him that he had become a little too friendly. He walked back to his desk, and said rather formally,

"I respect your loyalty and courage. Unfortunately they are misplaced. I shall see what can be done. Good day. Heil Hitler!"

When Leo Schmuelowitz arrived home, he was a sad sight. The hair shorn, the suit wrinkled and smelling disinfected, an eye swollen from a blow, he faced his wife trembling, helplessly embarrassed. His little daughter put a finger in her mouth, giggled and crowed, "Daddy, you look like a 'liminal.'"

They put him to bed and gave him some food.

Two days later he was on the train headed for the Dutch border to catch a boat in Amsterdam to Central America. Hilde and the little girl remained in Berlin.

The train was crowded with young soldiers who sang and talked tough. Leo made himself as inconspicuous as possible, sitting in a narrow passage on his suitcase, the only piece of luggage he had been allowed to carry along. The conductor came through and examined his ticket. Hardly looking at him, he mumbled, "Change in Hanover."

"What?" Leo was taken aback. "I thought this train was going direct to the border."

"Change of schedule due to military orders."

"How will I get to the border?"

"Inquire in Hanover." And he moved on.

In Hanover, Leo was told he would have a train to the border next morning at 5 o'clock. The problem was where to stay over night. It was getting dark already. He could not go to a hotel. They all had signs, "Jews not welcome." He did not dare to spend the night on a bench in the railroad station. A policeman might pick him up as a suspicious character. In a cigar store, he consulted a city directory, searching for Jewish sounding names. He decided to try his luck with Isaac Lewinsohn on Weidengasse 5a. Asking only elderly people for help, he was directed to a poor section of the city. It had begun to rain and it was completely dark when he finally rang the bell of a fourth floor apartment at Weidengasse 5A. The door was opened as far as the security chain would allow by a working man in shirtsleeves, and Leo explained his predicament.

"Please go away. It is forbidden to take Jews in." The voice sounded frightened.

"Listen, there is no danger for you. All I want is to get off the street. Let me sit somewhere in your place, and I shall leave early in the morning to catch a train to the border. I have a visa. I am all right."

"Who is there?" A woman's hand became visible.

The chain was unfastened and the door opened. A highly made up lady in faded finery and decorated with lots of cheap jewelry looked questioningly at Leo.

"He wants to stay overnight, honey," the man who had stepped back explained.

"Why not? Come in, sir." She had a high pitched rather sweet voice.

Leo entered. The walls of the hall were covered with photos of movie stars and actors.

"You will excuse me," the lady said with graceful formality, and disappeared.

"Come along. You can stretch out on the sofa in the living room," the man said, somewhat more friendly. "Maybe you would like something warm to drink?"

"No, no. Thank you. I will just sit here."

"O.K. Let me know when you want to leave in the morning." He left the room.

Leo looked around. In the dim light, he noticed the picture of a Madonna and in the china closet a tarnished silver goblet with a barely recognizable Star of David. He thought of Hilde. Was she safe? And the little one? Would he ever see them again? What in the world would he do in that Dominican Republic? He felt cramped and grew very uncomfortable, but did not dare even to shift his legs because the sofa springs creaked loud at every movement.

Leo tried desperately to stay awake. He checked his watch every few minutes, afraid to miss the early morning train. At four o'clock, he got up and knocked at the door through which his hosts had disappeared. The man came out immediately.

"Please let me out. I have to go now."

"You can't go yet. It is still dark. Jews are not allowed to be out at night here."

"I cannot help that. My train leaves at five. If I do not go now, I will miss it. Please unlock the door. Please."

"Herr Gott! You will bring us all into the KZ."

But he took out a key from the pocket of his bathrobe and opened the door just wide enough for Leo to slip out.

The streets were deserted. Luckily an early streetcar came by. He got on and reached the station in time for the train to the border. It had only three cars and there were few passengers. Leo entered quickly and with a sigh of relief, let himself fall on a seat. Two more stops and he would be at the border station.

He had dozed off but awoke with a start when the train came to a screeching halt. He let the window of the compartment down and leaned out to check the name of the station. An S.A. man who stood on the platform mustering the incoming train motioned to Leo.

"Hey, you, come out!"

Leo looked at him in disbelief.

"Who? Me?"

"Yes, you. You come out."

Leo got cold with fright. "What now?" he whispered leaving the car.

"Follow me!"

The man took him inside the station building. They entered a room that was bare except for a table and one chair. Leo thought, "Oh, God, are they going to beat me again?"

The S.A. man, an older man in a rather ill-fitting uniform, positioned himself behind the table and ordered, "Take everything out of your pockets and put it here on the table!"

Leo obeyed. One after the other, he put down a bunch of keys, a wallet, a handkerchief, a pocket watch, a small notebook—

"Stop!" the interrogator called. "Let me see that notebook. What is in it?"

"Just names and addresses."

"Addresses, eh? New York, Chicago, Paris, Buenos Aires. International Jewish conspiracy, I suppose?"

"Nothing of the kind. Just names of relatives and friends abroad. I have an official emigration permit. I thought some of these people might be able to help me."

"Yes, you Jews stick together. Now what is this here? Whom have you got in Munich? You know what happened in Munich?"

"No. What?"

"I tell you what. That is where they plotted against the Fuehrer. Who is this Alfred Springer in Munich?"

Leo began to perspire. He had absolutely forgotten who Alfred Springer was and why he had entered his name in the address book. He knew he had to think fast.

"It is an uncle of mine," he stuttered.

"An uncle?" the interrogator laughed sarcastically. "You can tell that to your grandma." He slammed the notebook on the table.

At that moment, the station master came into the room.

"Listen, Krauskopf, is this guy to go on this train or not? I have to give it the signal to leave now."

The S.A. man looked up and stared a moment searchingly at Leo. "O.K. Run!"

Leo gathered up the things on the table and stuffed them in his pockets. As fast as he could, he ran after the station master and reentered the train. He had just opened the door to his compartment when he heard his name called.

"Hey, Schmuelovitz."

"Not again," Leo cursed under his breath. "Oh God, not again."

Hopelessly, he went to the window. Outside stood Krauskopf, the S.A. man, raising his arm trying to reach the window. Leo wanted to retreat, but could not move.

"Here, Herr Schmuelovitz. You forgot your watch. Take it."

Leo took it.

The train started with a clanging bang; toward freedom.

On the following Saturday, the boat on which Leo Schmuelovitz was traveling was sunk in the English Channel.

THE HERO

The marriage counselor had earnestly advised them not to do it. The odds were absolutely against it. The macho tenor with the heavy brown mane, for whom teenage girls stood in line for hours before the opera house; and the feminist physicist with her energetic movements and short-cropped, though lovely, curls, who would have convinced Einstein to revise his Theory of Relativity. No way, do not do it! This was the counselor's verdict.

They had listened and nodded in regretful assent and then had gone and got married. How had Max and Moricia (funny name that!) got together at all one wonders? She had approached and persuaded him to sing at a benefit function of the Women's League. Arrangements had to be made for his appearance. They met to talk about a suitable hall and the program for the concert. They met again and more often than was necessary for the purpose, and they fell in love. They were astonished themselves that it had happened because they were well aware of the vast differences in character, interests and lifestyles that divided them. Nevertheles Max claimed that just as a ringing High C could bring the house down, love could move mountains. Moricia in turn proved with the laws of Newton and Mendel that it could not. So they sought professional counsel, and then disregarded it.

Things went surprisingly well, but arguments were frequent, noisy and almost violent. Soft and hard objects were thrown occasionally, and short periods of non-communication followed such blowups. Their disputes though were always of an intellectual nature. Last Saturday for instance was typical.

They had watched television together and seen women training for the army. The question came up if women should be allowed to participate in actual combat. Moricia was all for it. Max was horrified by the very thought.

"War is bad enought as it is. Women should not get actively involved. Disgusting," he shouted. "It is against women's nature. It will brutalize them, make them ugly and hard, unsex them and ruin their relationships with men."

"Oh, stop your nonsense," countered Moricia. "Women have become doctors and miners, pilots and astronauts. Why shouldn't they be soldiers?" And raising her voice, she cried, "All you men want us to do is use a broom or a vacuum cleaner, run a washing machine or diaper a baby. But we can handle a gun too, and fire a missile."

So one thing had led to another. The whole question of women's lib was drawn into the argument. Tempers got hot and hotter. There was some name calling and table banging. In the end, he had sat down at the grand piano and hammered out some operatic tune to drown out her voice, while she had turned away abruptly, giving him up as hopeless, and mounted the steps to the upper floor.

When she disappeared, Max stopped playing. There was a profound silence in the house. The argument seemed to be hanging in the air and made for an unhappy sadness-laden atmosphere. It was a relief when the sound of running water came from the bathroom upstairs. Max began to play again and to practice the difficult section of an aria, but his voice broke and he could not continue. He was staring at the music on the piano when he heard steps coming down. Surprised, he looked up.

There was Moricia standing at the foot of the stairs. A floodlight streaming from the ceiling showed her in all her loveliness. Dressed only in a half slip and a pink bra, she stood motionless, and with her eyes cast down like a penitent sinner, she said almost tonelessly. "There is a wasp."

Max jumped up from the piano stool and immediately taking manly charge of the situation, he inquired, "Where?"

"In the bathroom," came the answer, still in a very weak, subdued voice.

Resolutely he walked up to her. "Give me your slipper," he ordered. Obediently she took one off and handed it to him. Then she limped up the stairs showing the way. On the upper landing she explained, "It is in there" and entered the bedroom in a hurry, closing the door tight.

Max was left alone. The only comparison that came to his mind from his operatic repertoire was the scene in which Siegfried gets ready for the fight with the dragon. He opened the bathroom door carefully and slipped in.

There he was now all alone in the hot steamy silence ready to battle the beast. Slipper in hand, he looked around. No trace of it. With great misgivings, he lifted the shower curtain and looked behind. Nothing. He listened. No buzzing. Maybe Moricia had been mistaken. But then he looked in the mirror and saw the reflection of the wasp behind the soap dish.

It was in a deplorable condition, apparently half burnt from flying against the hot electric bulbs. But this was not the time for compassion. Raising the murder weapon, he made it come down with a terrible blow on the unfortunate intruder. Rather baffled, the victor looked at the victim and the additional casualties of a shattered soap dish and broken perfume bottle.

He tidied the place up as best he could and entered the bedroom to announce that the deed had been accomplished. It was completely dark in there, and from her side of the bed came the regular breathing of a relaxed sleeper. He was not prepared for this kind of reception and felt rather disappointed, like a knight whose lady fails to crown the victor after successful battle. He undressed quietly, lifted the covers and got into bed. Stretched out next to her, he stared in the dark at the ceiling. He thought and he wondered. Finally he turned to her, touched her shoulder and whispered, "I did it, Morey. That old wasp is gone."

She stirred, slung her arm around him, murmured, "My Hero!" and fell asleep again.

LOOKING IN

I am not exactly a religious man. I have a lot of doubts and I am rather lax when it comes to ritual observance. But there is one thing I absolutely believe in and that is the coming of the Messiah. I know there are those who are convinced that mankind is simply no good and that it is set on destroying itself and everything else. I cannot deny that there is a lot of bad in the world. But you can say what you want, it cannot shake my faith. I believe in the coming of the Messiah.

Therefore it should not be so surprising that when I met this man in the railroad station and he told me in the course of our conversation that he was the Messiah, I believed him. I must add though that I had been on the train all night, and while it was speeding through the darkness hour after hour, I had read a book on mysticism and gotten completely absorbed in it.

There was nothing extraordinary about this man who said that he was the Messiah. He was neither old nor young, neither thick nor thin, neither tall nor short. There was a compassionate smile on his face as if he were accustomed to pity people who would not believe him.

Of course I would not accept his claim unquestioningly.

"Are you coming or going?" I asked.

"I am afraid I am going," he answered.

"But if you are the Messiah, why are you not coming?"

He smiled his compassionate smile.

"I cannot come as long as there is idolatry in the world."

"Idolatry?" I asked astonished. "I thought that had ceased to exist a long time ago."

"It certainly has not. There is a lot of it around. I can prove it to you. And that is what keeps me from coming."

"You say you can prove to me that idolatry is practiced today?"

"I surely can if you will go with me."

My head was spinning from the long train ride. I was very tired and it was a snowy winter night. But I went with him. It was still dark and there were few lights in the houses. We had come into a suburb.

Suddenly my companion stopped.

"Have a look," he said and pointed to a brightly lit downstairs window of a nearby cottage.

I went closer and he followed.

It was easy to look in because the window reached down almost to the ground. It was an office-like room and a lady was sitting in front of a computer.

Strange things began to happen. The woman, who had stared deeply absorbed at the screen, manipulated some keys, and when the writing on the screen unfolded, her face lit up and her hands moved as if in silent applause. She consulted a book, which seemed to be kind of a magician's manual, and pressed some keys again. This time, after some uncertain flickering, the screen went black. The woman seemed taken aback in anger. She raised her fist as if she were ready to smash the machine and tore her hair in frustration. Finally she regained some composure, wiped a tear from her face, prayerfully raised her hands and made her fingers glide quickly over the keyboard. A moment of motionless suspense. Now the screen comes to life rolling down line after line. The woman is beside herself with excitement. She is throwing kisses at the computer. She is reaching for the magician's book to demand more miracles from the machine.

At this moment, my companion – the man who said he was the Messiah – taps the window. She hears it, but with a nervous jumpy gesture waves away the interruption. "Not now," her lips seem to form, "I am busy."

"You see," says the Messiah. "You see. Behold the idolatress! I cannot come."

I kept looking through the window at the woman before the computer. Was this man, whoever he was, was he right? Was this woman indeed an idolatress? Was this machine her God? Was she responsible for the Messiah's not-coming? Was she bad?

What a shame! So intelligent looking. In spite of the disheveled hair, such noble beauty!

I turned to my companion. I barely could see his compassionate smile. He was retreating and his snow covered figure was getting diffused in the white of the landscape.

But I could not take my face from the window.

"An idolatress," I whispered. "An idolatress."

Now a door opened and a young woman entered halfway. There was a strong resemblance to the lady at the computer. A daughter maybe. I felt almost sure it was mother and daughter. There was a mirror on the wall, so that the two could see each other. The daughter was beckoning to the mother, and the mother, with one last longing look at the computer, got up quickly. Embracing each other, they walked out together.

I turned around, but the Messiah was walking away faster and faster.

"You are wrong," I shouted after him. "You will have to come."

A RIDE

I noticed that the bellhop looked rather surprised when I asked if there was a bus going into the city. So I felt I had to explain. Somewhat shamefaced and apologetic, I informed him that since my wife had the car, I had to rely on public transportation. He accepted that and told me where to catch a bus.

At the bus stop, a few black people were sitting on a bench, waiting. They raised their heads a little when they saw me standing on my toes in a vain attempt to decipher the bus schedule. It made no sense, at least not to a "foreigner." The print had faded, and the space where the number of the bus should have been inserted was blank. I had been told that the bus ran hourly, so I considered myself lucky when it came soon. In order not to be rejected as had happened to me in New York, I had filled my pockets with change to have the exact fare ready.

It was a clever precaution. The driver had such an awe-inspiring beard and an equally formidable brushlike moustache, that he reminded me of a Prussian policeman before World War I, and made me feel like a schoolboy. Meekly I dropped my coins into the slot and was admitted.

What a terribly rough ride! I wondered if something might happen to my retina or my brain, some detachment or concussion. The vehicle seemed to have absolutely no springs. Later I found out it was a "Brummer," and I felt great relief knowing that I had sold all my Brummer stock recently.

Supposedly segregation does not exist anymore in the States. Not even in Florida. Therefore I felt extremely ill at ease when I discovered that I was being discriminated against. I happened to be the only white passenger on the bus, and not one black person, not one, would sit next to me. I smiled benevolently at all the mothers and their babies, of which there were quite a few. I am not exactly a baby lover, but I did not move when a tiny girl—just a few months old, but complete with hair ribbons and earrings—reached out for my glasses. To no avail. The mother simply shifted her position and pulled her away from me.

There I sat, alone, isolated, an outcast. The ride seemed endless. Up and down long hot streets, crisscrossing the colored neighborhoods. Everybody who got on or off seemed to have some destination. Perhaps bringing a child to the doctor; looking for bargains in a market; or going on a housecleaning job. Only I was clearly singled out, riding the bus as a map-consulting tourist who did not belong there and should have gone with a guided tour.

When the bus finally pulled into the crowded, noisy, loudspeaker-barking terminal, I got out in a hurry, trying to find solace and security in the white busy bank district.

It did not help. I still felt the stigma of being white.

A WALK

It is Sunday. Six o'clock in the morning. I am out for a walk. My doctor says it is essential for my health that I should walk. My wife does not believe in that. She is not overweight and besides no marriage is perfect. So I walk alone.

I am retired now. I have, as the expression goes, lots of time on my hands. I like that. I enjoy not having to watch the clock to fit in appointment after appointment. What business is it of yours if I was a doctor, a lawyer, a politician or a minister? I am retired and I have time.

The streets are deserted at this hour. Not even a jogger and rarely a car. I live on Hillside Street, and hilly it is. If Doctor Springfield wants to take a stress test and climb to the top of Hillside Street, let him! I am taking the car, and I will leave it on Live Oak Avenue, where it is flat and shady.

I like this neighborhood. I have lived in this city for over fifty years, and I know many people. These older houses are really quite attractive. Some of them regular mansions. Shit and Hell!! You can break your neck here. The pavement on this sidewalk has been broken for at least the last twenty years. I do not want to mention names, but that undertaker certainly made enough money to have the sidewalk in front of his house fixed.

Ah, here. Now that is different. You have to hand it to these Germans. I am tempted to use a pun and say they keep their property proper. The edges of the lawn cut neatly; the three cars parked like soldiers on parade. And their children. Everybody admires how well behaved they are. Still, that Hans got in trouble with drugs. So I guess you never know. As the Germans would say, "Es ist nicht alles Gold was glaenzt." In case you don't know German, it means "Not everything that shines is gold."

Why do I stop for the traffic light? Nobody is around but me. There is something eerie about traffic lights changing in empty streets. It reminds one of a clock ticking in a house laid in ruins by disaster; of eyes looking where there is nothing to see.

But here is somebody after all. Yes, I know them. That is the couple who are out Sunday mornings to collect cans. They stop at every trash bin or pile and pick out the grocery cans. They have a little cart, actually just a box on rickety wheels, where they put the stuff in. I wonder why they are doing it. To make a few extra pennies? They do not look that poor. Though I have never seen them driving a car. They are an odd couple. He, very tall with a full bushy beard; she, a short, fat cross-eyed woman, all the time talking loudly to each other as if involved in a hot but friendly endless argument. We know each other and they shout a greeting across the way from a distance. It echoes in the empty streets, and I return it somewhat embarrassed, in a low voice and with a slight wave of the hand. Poor folks!

These new glasses of mine do not do much for my vision. It has become almost an obsession with me to test my eyes on street signs. Of course I know it says "Essex Place." The letters on "Place" are too small. I better walk on.

That little rabbit sculpture on Dr. Harshley's lawn must be new. I did not expect him to care for that type of thing. Rather cute. Hey, wait a minute! It is real. Or is it? Slowly, slowly! I still do not know. It just sits there absolutely motionless. Well, we shall find out.

There he goes. Two jumps and stops again. Friend, I tell you, if you know what is good for you, hop along. If Dr. Harshley gets hold of you, you are liable to end up in his laboratory. I wonder where he sleeps. Not Dr. Harshley; the rabbit I mean.

The paper boys must have made their rounds in the dark. The bulky Sunday papers have already been fired on the lawns. There must be something of a kleptomaniac in me. I always feel the urge to pick up one of those papers. I know that the Maybaums are out of town. I could take that one along. Or at least read it here. We do not get the Sunday edition. Of course I do not do it. What an idea!

That motorcycle makes an infernal noise, disturbing the Sunday morning peace. It slows down. And a woman! She stops right next to me.

"Good morning, sir." Loud and robust.

"Good morning." A little hesitant and questioning.

"I have not seen you in a long time. You are out early."

"Yes. I am going for a walk."

"Walking is good for you."

"That is what my doctor says."

"He is right."

"I think he is. And how are you?"

"Just fine. Bill though is in the hospital. He had a slight stroke."

"I am sorry to hear that. How is he getting along?"

"Thank God. He is doing real well. I am on my way to bring him a bit of special breakfast. He likes that."

"I bet he does."

"How is your wife?"

"Getting along. Getting along. Her hearing is not what it used to be, and Dr. Springfield wants her to watch her diet because of her gall bladder."

"Well, give her my regards. I must go on. Nice seeing you. Goodbye."

"Good talking to you. I hope your husband will be all right soon. Stay well."

Off she goes in fumes and noise. To the hospital. To the sick husband. And who in the world is she? Probably one of the ladies who pass me at times, walking in pairs mostly, in shorts and so fast I wonder how their bosoms can stand being whipped up and down so relentlessly. She seems a good soul though, sincerely fond of her husband. I really should know her. Maybe it will come back to me.

The sun is getting higher, glaring over the trees. It is going to be another hot one. Just as well to go in now and pick up the car later. I could have walked a little longer if it had not been for the chat with that lady.

What are you lying around here for, Jack? You could have come with me so I wouldn't have to walk alone. He beats his tail three times, lifts his head a little, opens his eyes for a moment in lazy recognition and goes back to the business of basking and slumbering in the morning sun. Arthritis? You too?

And I enter the house.

THE MAGIC CANE

We had been known in town as the walking couple. The title was well deserved because hiking was our chief enjoyment. Not only did we walk all over town, we had climbed all the lower peaks in the New England mountains and even some of the higher ones. A nice hobby and a healthy one, especially when you come close to qualifying for senior citizenship. But then it had happened. Arthritis hit my wife's hip. She tried to ignore it but the condition got worse and painful. The doctor recommended the use of a cane as an alternative to pain-killing drugs that my wife hated to take. We were not enthusiastic about that suggestion but finally accepted it as the lesser evil.

It was the luckiest decision we ever made. Not that it helped too much in getting around, but it became a revelation of human nature. The cane helped to bring out the best in people. Not in us, mind you, but in those who saw us. I never knew how kind people really are until my wife started using the cane. It acted like a magic wand.

Have you ever tried to cross the street after a show in the Municipal Auditorium? Well, I have, and experienced all the frustration of the outraged pedestrian, murmuring curses against those inconsiderate drivers. But that is all a thing of the past. Now we rely on the Magic Cane. I take my wife by the arm, raise a warning hand against the oncoming traffic – and here we go, at a snail's pace, fearlessly straight across the road. All cars stop; drivers tip their hats, wave us on smilingly. A pleasure!

Who said New York redcaps are an unfeeling lot? No such thing. The other day we landed at Kennedy Airport. We had a lot of luggage and the weather was miserable, a driving rainstorm. Porters were at a premium. Finally I located one. Humbly I made my request to take our stuff to the bus stop. He grabbed the suitcases and took off in a hurry. I made a vain attempt to keep up with him. My wife was left behind altogether. Suddenly he turned around and in a voice half kind and half commanding said, "You go back to your wife. Tell her to take her time. I shall wait at the bus stop for you."

Oh, I almost forgot to tell you what had happened after our arrival at the airport. I had lost my wife. Why? While we were struggling along an endless hall in the crowd of rushing passengers, a good-hearted official had spied my wife, put her without my noticing it in a wheel chair, taken her to an elevator, and transported her by an esoteric shortcut to the entrance lobby. Since we had come from abroad, we had to pass customs inspection. Frankly, I almost regretted that I could honestly say I had nothing to declare. The customs officer took just one look at my wife's cane and then declared sweetly, "We cannot let the little lady wait. Here is your slip. Go ahead, and welcome home!"

You say our young people have little regard for the elderly and handicapped. Wrong again. On a nice Indian summer day, we had gone for a walk at the beach. It is about the only place where my wife can walk for a longer time without too much pain. To get back to the car, we had to climb a little sand hill. I had gone ahead to put the chair in the trunk. It was one of those access places where bearded boys and very sparingly dressed girls hang around smoking God knows what. When I returned to fetch my wife, I saw one of the girls helping her to come up the sandy incline, talking to her all the time cheerfully. A daughter could not have been more considerate and loving.

Doors do not need handles any more as far as we are concerned. Wherever we go, they seem to open by themselves and chairs are pulled up or exchanged for more comfortable ones in any restaurant or waiting room. Rides are offered so freely, we could almost garage our own car. Or we could rely on city buses. They will halt for us, bus stop or not.

But the medal of highest distinction for kindness belongs, I think, to the museum attendant who took me aside and whispered into my ear, "I would have offered her a wheel chair, but I was afraid she might be offended." How right you were, my friend! Who needs a wheel chair when you have a Magic Cane?

WELCOME HOME, HERMAN!

The two muscular ambulance drivers who, except for their friend-liness, could have acted as the giants in Wagner's "Ring," and who had driven me at breakneck speed from the hospital to my rural residence, deposited my mending bones carefully in a living room chair. It was a brand new recliner acquired by my shopping-wise wife at Sternfeld's in a water-sale after that memorable fire a month ago. Proudly she stood at my side wiping off a few tears, waiting for me to look around. I did and my eyes fell on a mini TV set, also a new acquisition. My kid brother, who just had turned 70 last Friday, was busy manipulating some of its controls; then he modestly stepped aside, and the show began. The screen lit up. There was a wild flickering of dots and lines. But finally they got organized, became steady and a message greeted me: "Welcome Home, Herman!" Now it was my turn to shed tears, and sniffing I managed to ask, "How in the world did you manage to do that, Fred?" – "Well," he smiled, "Fifty years ago you paid my tuition at the Technical Institute. It had to pay off sometime."

A memorable day. A new day, a different day. Fred left for his office, and Gilda busied herself in the kitchen. There was for a little while the clanging of pots and pans. And then there was silence. Silence. Do you realize what that means after weeks in the hospital? No more barking loudspeakers demanding the key to the drug cabinet; no more searching for Kathy because number 16 is in need of attention. No more clicking of heels in the halls and festive laughter at the nurses' station. Just silence. And unexpectedly a bird's call. Two notes. One low, one higher. Repeated three times? No four. Let me count. Not so fast! I cannot keep up with you, whoever you are. Now even five times. Amazing. I did not know they can vary their call like that. Some type of song sparrow I suppose. And silence again. Silence.

But in the afternoon it got lively. Neighbors dropped in; relatives and friends called. Gradually I assumed a new stature. As the story of my accident was repeated over and over again, sounding with every repetition more dreadful, I emerged as its hero. And why not? Had I not suffered enough? Look at me here propped up in the recliner, crutches leaning on one side. Rather helpless, wouldn't you admit?

That was the reason it was decided to call an aide for my assistance during the night. The agency we contacted recommended from its rich arsenal an elderly man, a sweet guy whom we certainly would enjoy.

He came as agreed in the late evening. It was a cold night. Therefore we were rather surprised at his attire. On the crown of his head sat a little straw hat, definitely a few numbers too small in size. A thickly padded jacket with a fur collar hid his face, except for a grizzly beard. But then again a pair of gleaming patent leather shoes surprised the astonished onlooker.

He introduced himself in a rasping wheezing voice as Michael Downhill, but encouraged us to call him Mike. Accustomed to accommodate himself to new surroundings, he entrusted a somewhat fatty bag to my wife, asking her to put it in the refrigerator for further reference during the night.

My brother and I were occupied in a simple card game. After Mike had been properly presented to us and given an abbreviated account of my accident, which seemed to move him genuinely, he looked around, found a comfortable sofa corner and installed himself as a voluntary umpire of the game.

From then on we did not have to worry. He knew exactly whose turn it was to deal and who had played which card. I am sure he even kept score without the need for pencil and paper. He visibly regretted it when we decided it was time to stop and go to bed.

He worked slowly, but methodically. He hung up my robe. He fluffed the pillows. I only noticed that all his actions were accompanied by a hoarse wheezing, as though it were hard for him even to pull a kleenex from the box.

My bedroom being rather small, I encouraged him to watch me from an adjacent larger room. But that seemed to be against his idea of professional responsibility. Instead he prepared for himself a comfortable chair near my bed, and after he had carefully doled out my various pills, again with his rasping, wheezing sighs, settled in the chair and covered himself with a little blanket. "I shall be right here when you need me," he announced.

We still chatted a little of this and that, of his family and of his car, of his job and of my past life. After a while, in the dim light that came through the window, I noticed that he had pulled the blanket over his head and had fallen asleep. Still, when I called him a little later, he responded promptly. Finally, exhausted from a long eventful day and helped by medication, I, too, fell asleep.

It was barely getting light when I awoke. I needed some help and called, "Mike." He did not hear. I had compassion on the man, but I needed help badly. So I became more urgent, "Mike, Mike!" Still no answer. In desperation I got hold of one of my crutches and barely reaching him, I poked his breast. His head fell down. Mike Downhill was out of reach. He was dead.

Regretfully, I peed in the bed.

VALIANT COWARDS

Longman closed the door quietly and stood motionless, listening to the dripping of the rain that came down steadily. So this was it. Now she was lying out there in her grave, the frail defenseless being. What would this weather do to her silklike silvery hair? He shuddered.

The funeral had taken place in the afternoon. Only a few friends had attended and when they offered to accompany him home, he had declined and told them he preferred to be alone.

He stood a while in thought. Finally shaking his head in somber wonder, he took off his coat, shook it out and slowly and methodically put it on a hanger in the closet. Then he entered the living room and reached for the light switch.

The kitchen door stood half-open. To his amazement, a light was coming and going as if the refrigerator door was opened and closed again.

Longman froze. Somebody moved around in the kitchen. He knew the sensible thing to do would be to make a loud noise, to run out and call for help. Instead he did not move and observed. And when the intruder, who seemed to be a young man, stood with his back to him drinking hastily from a soda bottle, he walked toward him and said softly, "Good evening." The man spun around, raised the bottle like a weapon, but dropped it the next moment, opting for flight. He tripped over a kitchen stool and took a heavy fall.

Longman told himself to leave the fellow alone and to run. He was no match for this youngster. Instead he went closer and asked, "Are you hurt?" The man murmured indistinctly, "No," but had trouble extricating himself from the stool and getting up.

Longman looked down on him but did not offer help. The burglar raised himself with difficulty. He looked rather neat in well-creased black pants and a dark shirt.

"So what will you do now?" he asked in apparent confusion.

"Nothing," said Longman. "I just buried my wife."

"Sorry to hear that," the man said with correct formality.

They stood for a while in silence. Then Longman said, "By the way, what is your name?"

A sputtering laugh came.

"You know I am not going to tell you that. Silly question. Just call me Joe."

"My name is Longman, Ed Longman. You hear, it's raining harder and harder. The water will get into the coffin soon."

The man who wanted to be called Joe was walking around in the kitchen irresolutely eying the back door. He was limping. Suddenly he stopped.

"I have to have some money." The voice now sounded dry and threatening.

"I never have cash in the house. Look." Longman pulled out his wallet and a little purse, and emptied them on the kitchen table. "Here. Three dollars and seventy-two cents."

Joe pocketed them quickly. "Well, let us look around. You must have something of value."

"Suit yourself. I do not think you will have much luck." Of all days today! Thank God she is not here. The shock would have killed her.

The robber had started walking through the house, Longman trailing behind. In the bedroom, he opened drawers quickly, making an expert search, discarding and throwing a lot of stuff on the floor. Ed watched horrified.

"Please do not do that! I cannot stand littering and disorder. Neither could she. She had everything so nicely bundled."

Again came the explosive sputtering laugh.

"Got any jewelry?"

"No."

"You sure?"

"I said no. Do not touch that velvet bag on the dresser, Joe!"

"Why not? What's in there?"

"My tefillin."

"Your what?"

"My tefillin. The phylacteries. My prayer straps. In the big blue bag with the Star of David is my prayer shawl. I am Jewish."

Joe withdrew his hand.

"I am Catholic," he said and crossed himself.

"I have a computer," volunteered Ed pointing to the desk in the den. "She gave it to me."

Joe walked over quickly.

"For a man who does not like littering, this desk looks pretty wild," he criticized. "Where is the computer? What, that? That is just a cheap calculator."

Nevertheless it disappeared under his shirt. He rummaged among the papers on the desk, then noticed the photo.

"Is that her?" he asked.

Ed nodded.

"That is a very fancy frame. Must have cost you a fortune."

"Well, yes. It is custom-made."

Joe picked it up and opened his shirt.

"Put it down! You cannot have that."

"Says who?"

"I say so,"

"All right. You can have the picture."

He tried to get it out of the frame.

"Stop it! You are going to tear it. Stop it!" He was yelling in hysteric excitement.

"To hell with your sentimentality!" Joe was shouting now too. He ripped the photo out of the frame. It tore and he threw the pieces furiously at Ed.

"That is enough," gasped Longman. "One should never bother with your kind. I will let the police deal with you."

He tried to grab the telephone, but Joe knocked the receiver out of his hand.

"Look how I can deal with your kind." And he produced a pistol from his trouser pocket.

"That is no threat to me." Ed's voice died down to a whisper, choked by tears. "Shoot! Shoot, by all means! I do not care any more."

Joe looked at him in contempt.

"Yes, and draw a twenty-year sentence. You are just a spineless worm."

Suddenly he turned and ran out the back door.

Aroused to new fury, Longman ran after him. It was useless. Joe had already disappeared in the bushes behind the house.

Out of breath Longman walked back slowly. With a last effort he slammed the door shut. What was he doing all this for? It was sheer nonsense.

Disgusted he looked at the disarray in the house, especially in the bedroom. Slowly he began to put things in order and discovered that the guy had taken much more than he had noticed. Never mind! He carried enough insurance.

Longman bent down to pick up the open handbag. The little mirror in the side pocket was broken. He straightened up, took out his handkerchief and blew his nose.

And the rain was still soaking her grave.

THE ARRIVAL

He looked around the room. There was nothing for him to do. He turned on the television, switched from channel to channel and turned it off again. He examined the pictures on the wall at which he never looked and now did not see either. Just stood there and stared. He stretched out on the sofa, but could not get comfortable because his legs were too long. He listened to some noises outside, got up, walked to the door, unlocked and opened it. A deserted street baking in the hot afternoon sun. He closed the door and checked carefully all safety devices. Finally he took up the telephone directory and turned to the Yellow Pages. He looked up the number of the airline and dialed.

"Valley Airlines, may I help you?" a pleasant voice answered. He felt sure she must be blond.

"Yes, you can. I mean I would like . . ."

"Would you like to make a reservation?"

"No, not exactly." He blushed and his speech got uncertain. "I-I just want some information."

"What do you want to know, sir?" a little impatient already.

"I need to know when the plane from Los Angeles arrives."

"Sir, we have six arrivals from LA daily. Which one do you want to know about?"

"Well, I'm not quite sure, but was there not one coming in around 5:30 p.m.?"

"Flight 713 L arrives at 5:27 p.m., if that is what you were looking for.

"Yes, I'm quite sure that is it. Thank you very much. Oh, Miss, . . . Miss, . . . excuse me, could you tell me, will the plane be on time?"

"Hold one moment please . . . Sir, yes, the plane is on time."

"Thank you, very, very much."

"Thank you for calling Valley Airlines."

He hung up and checked his watch. There were still two and a-half hours until arrival time. He sat down, but jumped up immediately. He went out, started the car with a roar and drove out to the airport. It took twelve minutes. He debated in his mind where to leave the car, and decided not to take chances with the hourly parking places, but to drive into the all-day parking lot.

He entered the airport building, walked up to the reception desk and looked at the arrival and departure timetables. There was not too much activity in the lobby, and a clerk, who had observed him a little while, asked him with a courteous smile if he wanted his ticket checked or needed somebody to bring in his luggage.

"No, no. Thank you. Just looking at the arrival times."

"The next arrival is from LA at 5:27. In about one hour and fifty-eight minutes."

"Yes. I know. I know."

He walked away from the desk quickly, found a men's room in a somewhat dark corner and entered. A sparkling clean, rather luxurious establishment. He relieved himself, washed carefully after he had, with some difficulty, figured out the working of the soap dispenser, and stood there alone listening. Because there was music piped in. Funny, he thought, to hear Beethoven's Ninth in this place. He wondered if he should lock himself into one of the stalls and listen undisturbed to the music, but thought it too much of a desecration and walked out.

He looked around and saw an escalator. He always hesitated to use one. He hated the getting on and stepping off. It made him dizzy. For a while, he was watching others using the moving stairway. Finally, when a little girl, a regular acrobat, hopped on it on one leg, he met the challenge, mounted, swayed, grabbed the handrail and was carried up to the observation lobby.

It was a circular, glass-enclosed hall. There were rows of benches, and people sat on them like in a theatre, watching the landing and taking off of little private airplanes. There was still ample time until the arrival from Los Angeles. He walked round and round. For a few minutes, he stopped to watch a soldier manipulating a slot machine. But when the man, who apparently had no luck and was losing, gave him a dirty look, he turned quickly and walked on. While he was examining the entrance to the different gates, a policeman passed and mustered him somewhat suspiciously. He felt so much like a criminal under this searching look, that he overcame his timidity and asked the attendant if he could pass into the waiting room behind the gate.

"Are you going to board a plane , sir?"

"No. No. I am just waiting for somebody."

"Somebody very dear, I guess." the man teased.

"Yes, indeed. Very dear."

"Well, I will let you go through, but you must stop for the metal detector."

So he waited and stopped, feeling like standing undressed in a doctor's office.

There were benches again, and he sat down. The little acrobat girl came and sat next to him. For a while they sat in silence. The girl was looking at him searchingly.

"Are you a flyer?" she finally asked.

"Oh, no. What an idea! I am just waiting for someone."

"I am waiting for someone, too."

"How come you are all by yourself? You should not be here alone. It is dangerous."

"That is all right. My aunt drops me off, and they all know me here. Nothing is going to happen to me. I am waiting for my mommy. She is a stewardess. Look! Look! There she comes. The plane is early."

She jumped up and ran to the window. He got up too, looked up and down and saw nothing. Until suddenly, with a tremendous roar, the mammoth plane shot by, screaming as it braked wildly to bridle its speed. Moments later it reappeared, creeping slowly toward the unloading ramp. All noise ceased. It now sat there heavy and silent. Still a pretty bird, but out of its element.

The plane door swung open, and in the opening a smart stewardess became visible.

"There is Mommy," said the child in a low voice, almost to herself.

One by one, the passengers came out. In the end, the stewardess came. Mother and daughter embraced and walked on. The girl seemed to have forgotten her new-found friend completely. But now, she turned around and shouted.

"Did nobody come for you?"

He simply raised his shoulders in a helplessly embarrassed gesture. He had known that there would be nobody coming for him.

REUNION

When I finally arrived at the place that in Jewish tradition is called "The World to Come," I found my mother there, as I had always expected. She was seated on a fragile golden chair, well suited for her slight build, and was turning the pages of an album that lay in front of her upon a billowing cloud. When I approached, she looked up and took off her glasses, which to my surprise she seemed to need even here. Her face that I remembered as always so serious and careworn was all smiles, and she extended her hand in a solemn, but heartfelt gesture of greeting. "What are you reading, Mom?" I asked.

She hesitated a little, but then let me look at the cover of the book. "Our Child" it said on it. "Oh, that one," I said, somewhat taken aback. "That is all about brother Eugene, and how cute he was as a little boy."

My mother wanted to say something, but I did not let her.

"Yes, yes. I know the story of how he wet his bed, and then said in sly defense, 'Oh, Teddy Bear has done it; he peed in the bed.' Very funny. I do not think I am even mentioned in the whole album."

The smile was gone from my mother's face. Half offended, half placating, she said, "You do not know what you are talking about. Of course most of it is about Eugene. After all, he was the first-born and got a lot of attention. But look, here are some photos of you."

"What about this one, in the sailor suit on the rocking horse? Is that me?"

"No, Bobby. That is Eugene."

"Of course."

"But this is you, just a year old, hardly able to stand – I think somebody had to hold you from the back – but already with that determined challenging attitude. And this one here. Look at that dignified bearing in your new outfit with the satchel, ready to attend the first grade."

"Well, let's not talk about school. It is a painful subject."

"Why? You were always an excellent student."

"That is what you are saying now, but you were never satisfied with what I did. With Eugene, it did not matter. With him, everything was alright, even when he barely passed. But with me, you were sitting on me even in pre-school.

"Well, I wanted you to succeed."

"Oh, is that why you slapped my face when my pen sputtered and made an ink blot on the paper?"

"You know I tried to erase it."

"But you made a hole and tore out the page. I had to rewrite the whole thing!"

"What else was there to do?"

I could see that my mother was growing uncomfortable, and I did not want to distress her. So I tried to change the subject. Noticing a bundle of neatly tied letters, I asked what they were. It was a mistake. I should not have asked. In an effort to hide them, my mother pushed them in the clouds in front of her. But I had already recognised the handwriting.

"What! You are keeping those? These are the letters from my girl-friend that you intercepted. You had no right to open and read them!"

"It was my duty as a mother to do it. From the contents it was quite clear that you had or at least planned to have intercourse with her, and I had to warn you against making her pregnant. You were only seventeen."

"Nonsense, I always used condoms!"

"So did your father, and still you were born."

"Really?"

"True enough," she admitted blushing.

"Conceived in overpowering passion! Oh Mom, how lovely!" And I rushed over to hug her.

For a while we were sitting in silence, holding hands. Then looking around I wondered, "Isn't Dad here?"

Again it was the wrong question. I could feel my mother's hand trembling in mine.

"I am sorry to have to tell you that temporarily he is down there."

"Incredible! I do not believe it. He never harmed anybody in his life."

"It is not that. But one night when he came home from a union banquet, he was definitely drunk. Of course I tried to hide the embarrassing occurrence from you boys. That's why you never knew it."

"Big deal. And for that he has to make time down there?"

"Well, alcoholism is considered a grave sin up here."

"Alcoholism! He just got a little tipsy once."

"That is all a matter of opinion. But he is permitted to come up here every Shabbos*, provided he makes Kiddush** over non-alcoholic nectar."

"Thank God for that!"

"You may get the opportunity to do that," my mother said solemnly. I felt the necessity of getting up and moving around a bit. There was a hallway nearby and all along were shelves with beautifully bound books. A plaque with ornamental golden letters

*Sabbath   **Sanctification of the Sabbath with a cup of wine.

proclaimed: "Classics, immortal." I began to examine the volumes, Homer, Shakespeare, Goethe, Dickens. Well, of course! And suddenly I stopped. "Mom," I shouted, but shocked by the echoing sound of my voice, I subdued it immediately. Rushing back to my mother, I whispered breathless, "Mom, did you know, I am among the classics, catalogued immortal?"

A tear ran down her cheek. "Of course, I know," she said. "But just imagine, if you had lived a little longer, you could have won the Nobel Prize."

"Maybe so," I muttered, "maybe so. But now I think I will go down and pay Dad a visit."

"Yes, my boy," my mother agreed, "that will be fine."

I went. It was a long descent and very dark. Finally I distinguished some kind of arched portal that led into a smoke-filled cave, and there they were sitting, Mr. Goldstein, Mr. Silberstein, and Mr. Diamant, all in shirtsleeves, busily absorbed in a card game. My father, with his back to me, was kibbitzing. At first, none of them seemed to have noticed me. But then, while shuffling the cards, Silberstein looked up and recognized me. Not too enthusiastic about the interruption, he continued shuffling, but at the same time touched my father's arm lightly with his elbow and grumbled, "Look who is here, George!"

My father turned around, rose and trying to penetrate the smoky darkness, shaded his eyes with his hand. I looked at him, and suddenly the scene changed. I saw myself as a young boy sitting bundled up in a taxi ready to be taken to the hospital for an operation, and there is my father's face, peering through the car window, shading his eyes to see me better. And now he raises his hand and spreading his fingers in the traditional gesture of blessing, I see his lips moving. I cannot hear him, but I know what he is saying.

"The Lord bless you and keep you." I lean back and feel safe.

Deeply moved, I went over to my father and took his arm. "You are coming with me. We are going upstairs," I said authoritatively.

"But Bobby," he resisted, looking back longingly at the card players. "Today is not Shabbos."

"Never mind," I replied, caressing his bald head. "Just hold your hand the way you did a moment ago, and I assure you, you will not need any pass."

And we ascended. My mother was all astonishment when she saw us.

"What a surprise!" she exclaimed. And then asked my father, "How did you manage to come up on a regular day?"

"Well," he answered with his famous left-eye twinkle, "Bobby made me give a signal that was worth a thousand passes."

It was not easy to convince my mother that everything was legal and aboveboard. There was a certain tone of mistrust in her voice when she said, "I only hope you were not again in the company of that Mr. Silberberg."

" -stein, Mother, -stein." my father corrected; "as a matter of fact, I was only kibbitzing."

"Come on, Mom," I intervened. "Do not always be so severe. A man must have a little fun sometimes."

I saw my mother's rigidness melt under my father's irresistible smile, that must have bewitched many a female. She moved and made room for him. He quickly sat down close to her, passing his arm around her waist.

I stopped an angel who happened to come by, and seemed to be a kind of heavenly tourist because he—or was it she?—had a camera slung over one wing.

"Would you mind taking our picture?" I asked.

"Certainly not. With pleasure. Get in!"

I took my position behind my parents, resting my arms on their shoulders. The angel snapped and immediately showed us the photo. It was lovely.

Too bad there is no way of sending it down for Eugene to see.

TESHUVAH (RETURN)

Moritz Bloch surely had seen better days. Only two or three years ago, he owned a small leather goods store in the German market town of Rachowitz, in the narrow street that winds from the market place to the synagogue. Short and a little too fat for his own good, he used to stand for hours in the entrance to his store, looking out with friendly, slightly tearing eyes through the oval shaped lenses of his old-fashioned steel-rimmed glasses. Affably, he would wink at passing acquaintances. In the case of an especially important citizen or valuable customer, he might slightly lift his stiff black hat, which generally sat way back on his bald head. When a customer tried to enter, he would deferentially make room for him, but as soon as he convinced himself that no major purchase was involved, he would let the tall pale clerk take care of the business.

Since the War, Bloch was a widower. In 1916, his wife had succumbed to an insidious disease. During the same year, his two sons had been killed in action on the Western Front. Those had been black days for this so sorely stricken man. For a long, long time, he had not been able to mention any of those dear names without shedding tears of his innermost sorrow. But as time went by, his basically easygoing nature made itself felt. His life reverted back to its old comfortable course, until the general economic collapse had affected him too, and forced him to give up his business.

It was in March of that year. It was still cold, but by noon it warmed up enough so that, in the streets of the small but busy town, the pavement of the roadways and sidewalks became visible under the mush of melting snow. When Moritz Bloch noticed this, he experienced a feeling of joyful satisfaction and reassurance. He knocked lightly with his cane on a snowfree spot as if to say, "Aha, there you are again. So you really managed to hide all winter under that thick rough ice cover without damage. What do you say, there is already a dry white spot. Yes, yes. Spring is coming in mightily."

But this lightheartedness did not last long. Too many serious worries burdened him. He just returned from the "Promenade" as the little city park was called which was a standard feature of the towns of that region. While taking a walk there, he had figured out that the small capital that had been left after the closing of his business would be used up in a month's time and that it was a complete mystery to him on what he would subsist afterwards.

He stopped in front of the show window of a cigar store and looked at the display for a good while. But he was not, as usual, attracted by the fatbellied, lightly powdered cigars with their showy golden paperbands, that his sons as little boys had loved to put as rings on their fingers. What aroused his interest was a fanshaped display of lottery tickets, and the sculpture of a bearded dwarf, his face distorted by a grotesque expression of wild joy, pouring a stream of gold coins from a bag.

Moritz Bloch smiled. Well, Well! He could not expect to win the jackpot right away. But two, three thousand marks might come his way some time. Absorbed in thought, he walked on. Would it not be the limit of irresponsibility to risk his last pfennig for a vague hope? What actually were his chances of winning? He turned and went back to the show window once more. But there was no chart that could tell him anything. With some effort, he had already pressed his cane under his left arm and put his right hand on the handle of the store door, when he suddenly stopped, shook his head as if dissatisfied with himself, said rather loud and audibly, "Nonsense!" and stepped back. But he had barely walked twenty feet down the street, when he abruptly turned around and now, determined and walking quickly, entered the store. Slightly out of breath and clearing his throat frequently, he asked and paid for a lottery ticket.

In the past, Moritz Bloch had not been too diligent a *schulgoer**. But now he was seen in the synagogue with great regularity at Friday night services as well as Saturday mornings. People though did not see anything out of the ordinary in this change of habit. They simply figured now that old Bloch had no business, he turned again to the customs and rituals of his fathers and used his ample leisure to practice them. Bloch himself most likely would have explained this sudden religiosity in a similar way. It is even quite possible that he would not have thought about it at all, had he not been stirred by an unusual experience.

It happened during a Friday night service. The congregation had just turned from facing the Ark toward the entrance doors in order to usher in the advent of the Sabbath with those graceful verses that compare this hour to the greeting of an entering bride. Like everyone, Bloch stood facing the entrance. On the lenses of his glasses, the lights of the candelabra that hang from the ceiling left a festive reflection. At that moment, he saw an apparition. It did not force itself upon him in a dreamlike fashion; it was more a creation of his own mind. The center door opened and the mailman who daily delivered Bloch's mail entered in the attire of a sexton. He walked down the center aisle, halfway, stopped and proclaimed with cantorial sing-song, "Moritz Bloch has won 50,000 marks in the lottery."

*One who goes to the synagogue regularly

Bloch left the sanctuary before the service was over. He was in an angry dispute with himself. Was that what his God had deserved from him? Had he, an old, honest merchant, sunk so low that he believed he could make cheap deals with the Almighty: insincere piety in exchange for lottery winnings? He felt his face get red-hot with childlike shame.

But as time went by, he looked at the whole affair in a different light. It seemed to him that he was entitled to some restitution from God. After all, did He not make him lose his wife and his two promising sons? And had he, Bloch, not suffered the loss without rebellious murmuring, only in sincere sorrow? Was it too much to expect that now since he had gotten to this stage of poverty, he would be rewarded with a modest provision for his old age? Consequently he felt that he could afford to ask God to favor him in his lottery gamble.

After the strange vision on that memorable Friday night, he had stayed away from the synagogue for a while. But now he attended again with punctual regularity and prayed with all the fervor that his slow temperament would allow, asking to win enough money that would assure a carefree old age or at least a few quiet years. He went even further. In an almost militant mood, he took up the practices of his youth: he put on *tefillin*(phylacteries), and recited prayers every morning—all this filled with the sole idea that by complete concentration he could force his luck.

Every day around noon, he went for a walk on the "Promenade" and invariably ended up in the cigar store where some time ago he had bought the lottery ticket. He selected a cigar and standing on tiptoe to reach the always burning open gaslight on the counter, he lit it pulling noisily on the cigar. With lips tightly closed around it, breathing heavily and not looking at all at the store owner, he asked if the list of winning tickets had arrived. With a quick experienced glance, he searched for his number, but found again and again that it had not been drawn.

His hope sank more and more. Nearly all the prizes had already been announced. The last drawing was scheduled for a Thursday. On the following day, Friday, Bloch prolonged his walk longer than usual. On his way home, contrary to his custom, he avoided the side of the street on which the cigar store was located, and entered the little kosher restaurant where he generally took his noon meal. As always, after he had eaten, he immersed himself in the daily newspaper, but hastily turned the page when he unexpectedly came across the headline "Last Lottery Drawing Day." He ordered a cup of coffee and spent the next couple of hours watching a chess game in which two patrons were absorbed. Bloch did not know them. Besides he understood nothing about chess.

The sun was going down when he came out on the street. Here and there, a few Jewish men were already walking slowly, festively attired, to the synagogue. Moritz Bloch now rushed directly over to the cigar store. The owner greeted him, remarking jokingly that he had already missed his customer. He offered him the open box from which Bloch generally selected a cigar. But today, he declined. "No, no. I do not smoke now. I just wanted to have a quick look at the list of the last lottery drawing." With unruffled courtesy, the store owner spread it out before him. Bloch skimmed the group of figures which could be important for him. At a first cursory glance, he could not find his number. Maybe he had missed it? He forced himself to remain quiet. With his thick fingers, slightly trembling from emotion, he tried to keep the lines apart and went down the columns examining every single number. No, his number was not there. His ticket had not been drawn. He had won nothing. He felt as if all life had left his body and he was standing there as an empty shell, icy, devoid of all feeling. He could barely, with a forced laugh, get out the words, "Well, no good. At least not for this time," and walked out dragging his feet heavily.

So that was it! God had cheated him. In vain his supplications. In vain the mention of the tragic loss of his wife and sons. In vain the regular attendance at the synagogue and the punctual recital of the prescribed prayers. Well, he for one now knew what to think of this "Just God." Fickle was His rule. Sometimes boundless favoritism; sometimes heartless disregard. But this much he knew: he, Moritz Bloch, would not enter the synagogue anymore. His hands would not touch *tefillin*; his lips utter no prayer.

Passionately talking to himself, he was unaware in which direction he had been going. And so he noticed with no little astonishment that he was standing in front of the synagogue where the Friday night service had just started. He was about to pass by quickly in order not to meet any acquaintances, and possibly be asked to enter with them, when he felt an irresistible, almost blasphemous urge to enter the temple in spite of everything. Much as his reason resisted, a mystical force seemed to draw his feet toward the entrance portal. And before he really knew what he was doing, he was already sitting in his customary seat in one of the back rows.

A turmoil of thoughts and feelings agitated his mind. Shouldn't he storm to the front, mount the *bima* (altar) and open everybody's eyes about the "trustworthiness" of their "Just God." It would create a terrible commotion, but he would offer irrefutable proof so that all would be silenced in shame. Challengingly, he looked around, but nobody took notice of him. Softly murmuring, all were busy with the reading of a silent prayer. Moritz Bloch grew somewhat uncertain when he noticed how the service continued completely undisturbed, quietly following its ordinary course. His agitation abated under the influence of the soothing warmth that the familiar surroundings radiated. And he began to think anew.

Jubilantly rose the Sabbath Psalm, *Mismor Shir*, rendered by the strident voices of the boys choir, perhaps not to perfection, but surely with all the enthusiasm at their command. Moritz Bloch listened impressed. Could he be mistaken? Shouldn't the One to whom children lift up their voices so clear and carefree be Himself absolutely pure and holy? Should anybody even dare to argue with Him? Was it not more than enough that He allowed His faithful ones to worship Him with tradition-honored customs, to sing to Him in festive awe and grateful joy? And to find uplift and strength in the holy service for Him? Humming in a low voice, he took up the melody of the Sabbath Psalm. Shame and confusion overcame him like on that Friday night when he had left the temple mortified by the profane vision of the announcement of his win in the lottery. When the last words of the *Veshomru*, "He rested and was refreshed," softly trembling, ebbed away, his eyes were filled with tears. In childlike simplicity, the old man regretted his error. Hardly anybody became aware of Moritz Bloch's strange emotion. The few who noticed something thought he most likely was observing the *Yahrzeit* (Anniversary of Death) for his wife or one of his sons.

But old man Bloch suddenly felt quite young and light. He could not have told if what he felt now was true religiosity. He only knew that a nightmarish oppression had been taken from him, that his soul was freed from that blasphemous power that for months had forced him into unnatural reward-demanding piety. His body that quite out of character with his nature had become rigid, relaxed. The features of his face that ever since he had bought that fateful lottery ticket had taken on a hard, obsessed, almost malicious expression, softened, and his eyes began to smile again, slightly tearing in happiest contentment. He was not bothered by the question of whether he had found his God in this rare hour. He was satisfied by the consciousness that he had settled his accounts with Him. During the final hymn that the boys shouted out in a happy tune, he had the impression that his hand was taken and forcefully shaken as a token of a finally accomplished reconciliation.

Wonderfully elated, Moritz Bloch left the synagogue. Nothing could happen to him anymore. He had again become his own self, simple and true, free from troublesome thoughts and doubts which were more than he could manage.

In his high-spiritedness, he walked on and on, although it had started to rain, until by sheer habit he reached the "Promenade," the place of his former daily walks. The old man had hastened along too quickly; his face was sweaty; a panting whistle came from his open mouth. The raindrops on his glasses made the street lights dance in a prismatic broken glitter before his eyes, and obstructed his vision. Moist hot waves went through his body; heart cramps made the pulse hammer in his neck; he felt nauseated and dizzy.

Thus it happened that when he ran into a group of drunken fellows, he did not know exactly where he was and whom he was facing. The group, noisy and mischievous, blocked his path and did not let him pass. At this point, old Bloch's mind got mixed up. What did these people want from him? Had they come to upset the equilibrium that he had restored with such painful effort? Did they want him to plunge again into that nightmare of insincere obsession? A furious rage overcame him. No, by God! He would not let them rob him of his peace of mind without a struggle. Completely beside himself, he shouted, "I am a poor merchant, but an honest one. Yes, all my life, I have been honest and the few months of my straying do not count anymore since today, do you understand? And now, I do not want anything but quiet. Poverty and quiet!" He had raised his closed fists with which he had beaten time in the air to his last words, and stood there as if ready to fight. It was his good fortune that the rowdies who surrounded him concluded that the foolish oldster probably was in the same condition as they. So, after they had stood there a moment stunned by his unexpected vehemence, they took the thing as a big joke and broke out in uproarious laughter.

But Bloch did not seem to see them anymore. As if he had won a decisive victory, he turned away well satisfied with himself and smiling contentedly was soon gone in the darkness of the park.

GODFATHER DEATH

To say that he looked like Death itself would have meant paying him a compliment. Even in its representation as scythe-bearing skeleton, Death shows an inexorable sovereignty, or at least the scornful laughter of the eternally triumphant. But Siegfried Trendel's sorry appearance only showed the lamentable decay of a human body that indeed could call to mind the popular personification of the Grim Reaper. His occupation consisted of the care of the dead in the Jewish Congregation. As the most active member of the Burial Society, the *Chevra Kaddisha*, a sinister aura surrounded this man with his toothless mouth, the tearing eyes and the sallow cheeks under the black dusty slouch hat. He had become so familiar with Death that he was able to meet mourners with absolute equanimity even under the most heartrending circumstances.

It is commonly known that truckdrivers, actors, ministers talk shop whenever they meet. So Trendel. He had only one subject of conversation, Death, and that with all the technical details as they related either to dying itself or to the ritually correct treatment of the dead and the laws of mourning for the bereaved. It might even happen that in times when the Jewish community had been spared for a while, Trendel would show some interest in the passing of non-Jewish people, although only in theory. In other professions, such a zealous attitude may be considered praiseworthy, but in

Trendel's sad business, it seemed grotesque. No wonder then that when spoken of, he was often given the uncharitable nickname of *Neshome-Khopper*, which is Yiddish for "soul-snatcher."

It was part of his business practice – if it can be called that – to go and see the terminally ill, paying them the tradition-hallowed meritorious sick call. He seemed to imagine the danger of some competition, and mildly suggested to the family his availability should his services be needed. For Trendel, the principal purpose of these visits was to ascertain if the patient really was on his last legs, because in this respect he stubbornly trusted only his personal experienced judgment.

In the exceptionally hot summer of 1926, during which several cases of typhoid fever had occurred in the city, the nine-year old daughter of Attorney Walter fell ill, and became so critical that the chance for her recovery seemed very poor. Since Walter was a well-known personality, not only as a trial lawyer, but also because of a number of honorary offices he held in the community, it was not surprising that the progress of the child's sickness was followed with general interest. With the morbid haste that finds enjoyment in anticipating impending doom, the town gossips already spoke of the terrible blow the parents would experience if they had to lose Ruth, their only child. Admittedly though, in this case, the general interest and regret were sincere because the pretty, well-mannered girl was well liked by everybody. Unfortunately the news of the condition of the young patient continued to be serious.

Consequently Trendel decided not to delay a visit to the Walters and to form his own personal opinion of the case. He felt entitled to do that because he occupied a little attic apartment in the lawyer's house and occasionally received little gifts from him. This latter practice was followed by a good many others. And for good reason. People felt guilty for the low economic condition of this man who diligently fulfilled an honorable religious duty, but at the same time was the butt of some poor jokes about his zealousness. Besides there may have been an unconscious attempt to propitiate destiny because of Trendel's close association with death.

At first Trendel's strategy was not successful. He had rung the bell at the Walters at different times to inquire after the child's health, and indicated that he would like to visit. But the maid who opened had refused him entrance every time. Nevertheless he repeated his inquiries almost daily and about a week later he had his chance.

On the stairway he met the doctor who had taken charge of the case. Professor Silberberg, with whom Trendel had occasionally come into contact in his ritual business dealings, was a famous authority, but old-fashioned enough to make housecalls. He was climbing the stairs behind Trendel. Tapping his shoulder, he asked jovially, "Well, Mr. Trendel, always chipper?"

"Ah, Professor Silberberg," Trendel stopped to lift his slouch hat, "nu, Thank God, I cannot complain, knock on wood!" And he touched the banister. "I suppose you are going to the Walters?"

With marked fitness, he tried to keep up with the hurrying physician. Seeing his opportunity, he said, now rather out of breath, "By the way, I myself had the intention to look in on the little one. After all, one lives in the same building."

"Well, why not come in with me for a moment?"

The door to the Walter's apartment had already been opened, and the doctor greeted the waiting parents, whose careworn faces were lit up today with a ray of hope that they hardly dared to express. Professor Silberberg addressed them in his lively way.

"Well, how are things going? A little better, you think? That is capital. Here, good Mr. Trendel wants to say 'hello' to our little patient, too."

It was impossible to raise objections since Trendel appeared now under such high protection, and so they all jointly entered the sickroom.

The windows of the spacious room were darkened, and with a faint hum, a fan stirred an aircooled breeze. The bed was put up hospital-like, so that it could be approached from both sides. Here then lay the pitifully emaciated child, who, raised to an almost upright position, looked with wide open eyes at the professor.

There is something magical about the effect that the entrance of a renowned physician can produce. Changed is the limp obscure atmosphere that for hours has been hanging in the room like a heavy cloud of sighs and dried-up hope. Forgotten is the torture of the endless night, blown away pain and complaints. All is strength, confidence, trust.

Professor Silberberg's appearance was of the type to enhance this effect greatly. Light and vitality radiated from his tall, almost soldierly figure. The intelligent, scholarly face, the large cool hands with their finely marked veins inspired at the same time confidence and respectful admiration. If there was, as is often the case with important personalities, a certain aura of inaccessibility around him, it disappeared the moment he began to speak. All severity left his face and the many wrinkles around his eyes and mouth pronounced a friendly, warm interest.

"Well, Ruthie, how are you doing today?"

"Thank you, pretty good."

Weakness and modesty made the answer almost inaudible. As was his custom, the doctor began to chat a bit before proceeding to the examination.

"You know, you are lucky that you can lie here in the nice cool room. There is a terrible heat outside, even worse than the days before."

"Really?"

"Yes, awfully hot."

While talking he had unnoticed taken her hand and felt the pulse. Suddenly she raised herself completely. Pushing her arms into the pillows behind and stretching her head forward, she stared into the dark background of the room.

Trendel, who had modestly stopped at the door as quiet observer, now stepped forward. Not in the least embarrassed, he approached the child's bed. Apparently he intended to smile, but his face just turned into an ugly grimace. With his slightly trembling hands, he tried to stroke her cheeks.

"Don't you know me anymore?"

"No, go away!" She pushed his arm away and leaned back into the pillows. The scene got extremely awkward, and the mother tried to straighten things out.

"Look, Ruthie," she said with mild, but firm reproach. "You know Mr. Trendel from upstairs."

Accustomed to obedience, the well-bred girl apparently was ashamed of her discourteous behavior.

"Yes, I do," she whispered, but remained lying motionless and frightened.

Professor Silberberg, who saw that the child was still upset, quickly put an end to the disagreeable incident. With slight impatience, he declared that he now wished to examine Ruth and sent the father and Mr. Trendel out of the room.

Understandably Mr. Walter was in no mood for conversation with the latter. He was afraid the shock, though unfounded, might upset improvement of his little daughter. In silence and rather business-like, he led Trendel into his study. There he offered him a cigar, put three more in his pocket, and waited for the unwelcome visitor to take his leave. But Trendel was in no hurry. He bit off the tip of the cigar and picked up a lighter from a little table that stood next to the massive desk of the lawyer. Walter had no choice but to sit down and start a conversation.

Ill-tempered as he was at the moment, he could not resist the temptation to needle Mr. Trendel by asking how business was these days. He could not have touched a more sensitive nerve. The old man was accustomed to be treated with respect, even if it was bestowed somewhat unwillingly and mixed with fear and poorly disguised disdain. He demanded that people pretend to believe that he fulfilled his sad office only for honor's sake. To make fun of it and to treat it as any ordinary occupation he considered an insult, and rightly so, because in his way he was a pious man. Mockery he would not tolerate, even if it came from a benefactor of the upper class. And so, getting more and more excited, he showered Walter with a flood of reproach.

What did the "esteemed" attorney mean by his ironic question? Did he wish to offend him and to ridicule his religious activities? As far as he knew, nobody had ever found anything dishonorable in them. Surely there were nicer and pleasanter occupations, and Mr. Walter seemed to be unaware of the fact the he, Trendel, too, had been in an ordinary business at one time. That, as a merchant, he had not been as fortunate as other people, for that he was not to blame. What of it, if in the course of time, he had dedicated himself exclusively to his present pious occupation. It was well known that, also in his better days, he had always been ready to perform the last act of kindness for the dead. Were not people needed for this service, especially since, as everybody knew, the "higher-ups" did not particularly care to have much to do with those things.

Mr. Walter was taken by surprise. He had not been prepared for such an outburst from the generally servile man. Greatly embarrassed, he tried to excuse his ill-mannered behavior.

Mr. Trendel should by no means think that he had intended to offend him. Nothing could be further from his mind; absolutely nothing. And he continued to apologize, moved quite likely by the subconscious fear that evil consequences might ensue should the old man depart in anger. At this moment, voices in the hall indicated that the doctor was about to leave. Walter, who was anxious to say goodbye to the physician, tried to speed up the reconciliation with Trendel by taking some banknotes from his wallet. But the old man remained stubborn and did not want to accept anything. Walter had to force the rather substantial gift on him.

At the goodbyes in the hall, Trendel was also honored with well chosen words of thanks by Mrs. Walter. But he had not much use for her social graces and easy cordiality. He was too well acquainted with that smooth attitude and acknowledged it only with a mumbled response. Compared with her, he readily gave preference to the lawyer and his unmistakable "language." So he hardly waited for her to finish. Instead he turned again to Mr. Walter and parted with the relatively friendly pronounced consolation that all was in God's hand.

So it happened that the two unequal men who had come for very different purposes met again while leaving. Trendel, who should have climbed up to his attic, would not pass up the opportunity of accompanying Professor Silberberg for a bit. Explaining that he had to go on an errand, he started a "professional" consultation with a sigh. "*Nebbich* (What a pity!), the poor child."

"Yes, she has had much to suffer."

"Nu, she wouldn't have to suffer much longer," lamented Trendel, pushing his hat up his forehead and wiping off the sweat.

"How do you mean?" asked the Professor somewhat hurried and looking around for a taxi. The heat was unbearable, but Trendel, who hated to have the conversation interrupted, stopped in the hot sun and putting his hand on the doctor's arm to get his attention, uttered, "That child will not make it."

Professor Silberberg, who had found some shade under the marquee of a shop window and was still searching for a cab, replied that with God's help, he hoped to get little Ruth well. The old man shook his head in unbelief.

"That child, not. That child, not." he repeated almost singing, with a disagreeably arrogant smile on his face.

Piqued by Trendel's unreasonable insistence on his pessimistic prophecy, the professor now got indignant.

"My dear Mr. Trendel, for God's sake, will you kindly tell me why you are so interested in the child's death?"

"Interested? Who is interested? I have seen the child. I know."

"How can a pious man as you talk like that! You must admit I have stood at sickbeds often enough. I know pretty well what death looks like. The child is weak. But with proper care, she will surely recover. The sickness itself is abating; it is the weakness it has caused that probably deceives you."

"My dear professor," Trendel's mouth was twisted again into his sour smile of superior knowledge, and he even took the liberty of giving the doctor a few light taps on the shoulder, "I am now working for 37 years in the *Chevre.* I know who will die and who will not."

Professor Silberberg, who had just succeeded in stopping an empty taxi, could not help laughing. "You really are an incorrigible pessimist."

Seated in the car, he reached for Trendel's hand, shook it, and said, "To tell the truth, I do not see why you should be such an expert on death prognoses. Usually you come when everything is over."

The starting car threw him gently into the upholstery, and still laughing and shaking his head in wonder over the old man's stubborness, he drove off. But Trendel, greatly offended by the doctor's flippant tone, yelled after him with all the might of his broken hoarse voice, "Well, we shall see!"

In the not too large congregation of a medium-sized town, nothing remains secret. One knows every family and takes special interest in the doings of the wealthy and the congregational employees. Of course one is better informed about the private life of the rabbi than about that of the *shammes*, but even the latter can not do anything without being subjected to the comments of the congregants. Consequently Siegfried Trendel too could not fall sick without it being discussed by a number of families at the dinner table. One might have expected that even the news that the shaky oldster had permanently bowed out of this world would not have greatly affected his coreligionists. But that was not so. Trendel was as familiar a sight as the clock on the courthouse or the war monument. It was taken for granted that he would trot busily through the streets, regardless of heat or cold, seemingly unaffected by rain or snow, that old and young, rich and poor could be prepared for their last rest only with his direction and cooperation. Due to his job, people seemed to forget that even he was not immortal, and that one day, he, too, would be in need of those same services that he was accustomed to render to others. Also Trendel had apparently forgotten that. He was one of those tough characters who enjoy robust health, although they look as though they could not last the next three days. His sickness was absolutely incomprehensible to him, and he was not prepared to take it seriously. The rattling and whistling in breast and bronchial tubes were nothing new, and he had always coughed and expectorated. That was no reason to run right away to a doctor. Most of them were probably charlatans anyway.

"As long as one smokes, one lives," he retorted to his *Chevre* brethren, who frequently came to look after him and advised him to cut down on his smoking. But the laughter that was meant to accompany this, his favorite saying, sounded more and more like a hoarse bark, and he gasped for breath. Different doctors were recommended to him, but he simply drew a thick woolen sock tight around his neck, declared that the downpour at the schnorrer Goldstein's funeral was to blame for all this, and insisted he would be all right in a week.

This did not happen, but Trendel remained his old stubborn self. He tried this and that home remedy and did not want to hear anything of professional medical help. Attorney Walter was treated abominably when he personally came to inform Trendel that he – at his own expense of course – had asked Professor Silberberg to have a good look at him and to order what was needed. Instead of a single word of thanks, Trendel shouted at Walter in hot rage, "He is the last one I want. You can cancel that immediately. I can give you that in writing, this man does not come near my bed."

Like an obstinate child, he turned around in his bed and showed his back to his worried benefactor. No wonder Mr. Walter felt insulted by this unreasonable and aggressive behavior and with "Well then, leave it," slammed the door and left.

But why this bitter resentment against the professor on the part of Trendel? One can only assume that it was related to little Ruthie's recovery that had come about in the meantime. Was he really such a horrible soulsnatcher that he begrudged the girl the young life she had fought for so hard? Or did the disappointment of seeing his prediction not come true make him bare of all humanity? To be fair one must bear in mind how wrapped up Trendel was in his profession. Basically he had nothing against Ruth, the professor or anybody else (although his dull life did not allow for much friendly caring either), but he felt that his professional reputation had been affected by his wrong prognosis. Probably the doctor would have felt the same way if things had gone the other way. As it was, Ruth's healthy appearance was a constant irritant to Trendel, and his only consolation was the fact that she was unaware of his mistaken prediction. But as far as the professor was concerned, he could not stand the idea of having been made a fool. And so he bore him a grudge, as bitter and unreasonable as only he could do it.

One morning Trendel was standing at the kitchen sink, trying to wash up. In his shirt and underwear, he was a deplorable sight, and the effort made him cough almost constantly. He, who had been so confident, now shook his head confused and worried by the force of the attack. He was just about to return with halting steps to his bedroom, when the bell was rung impatiently. At the same time, there were loud knocks at the door, and Trendel's name was called by an excited breathless voice. He opened as fast as he could and in bolted the *shammes* of the congregation. The always-hurried and busy man was completely beside himself. Gasping for air, he fell on the kitchen chair. "Who do you think has died?" he managed to ask with a last effort. But before Trendel had had a chance to guess and so to diminish the impact of his terrible news, he gave the answer himself, "The Judge!" That was the president of the congregation.

Only now the *shammes* allowed himself to catch his breath and to take a glass out of the kitchen cabinet that he filled with water and gulped down quickly. Then he sat down again, waiting for the effect that his news was sure to produce. It is doubtful that Trendel ever in his life had lost his composure the way he did now. "Boruch dayan ho-emmeth"* he stammered, wringing his hands. "For Heaven's sake! Why? Absolutely sudden? Come on, tell already! What a thing, unbelievable!"

"Yes, stroke, this morning."

Trendel stared speechless in front of him. "When will the body be picked up?" he finally asked thoughtfully.

The *shammes* jumped up and looked at his watch. "At noon. I must rush. By the way, he will be taken out to the cemetery in a horse-drawn hearse, not in an automobile. You know, for greater solemnity."

"But we don't have a wagon hearse."

"Well, I will just have to borrow one. That can be arranged. But I have to go now. I only ran up here because I thought you would be interested. How are you getting along yourself? In all this commotion, I forgot to ask. You are still coughing much too much. Hurry back to bed! Goodbye!"

When the sexton had left, Trendel walked back to his room, holding on to furniture wherever possible. Sitting on the edge of the bed, he was lost in thought. Now the Judge too. Who would have expected this to happen so suddenly. Such an honorable man. Of course he was not without faults either, but all in all . . . As far as he himself was concerned, he had always treated him with proper respect. He could easily have lived for another fifteen years. He must say it was nice of the sexton to take the trouble of coming to tell him all about it. With horses, they would convey the body

*"Blessed be the just Judge." The ritually prescribed response to the news that a death has occurred.

85

to the cemetery. Very good. The man deserved some special treatment. Trendel is not for motorization of burials anyway. Oh, the attendance that will draw. Simply everybody will turn out. And he, Trendel, he would be missing? Who will officiate instead? Simonsohn perhaps. He isn't bad, but still much too young for such a prominent funeral. No, no; they will have to leave the honor to that fat Glogauer who sometimes substituted for him before, although under his command, almost everything goes wrong; especially when it comes to lifting the coffin into the hearse, it never goes smoothly. By rights, there is only one to whom the proper execution of a ceremony of such proportion can be entrusted and that is he, Siegfried Trendel. And suddenly he had made up his mind. At twelve o'clock he is going to be at the house of mourning, and from there on will take charge of the procedings as he had always done it. Let it sting and prick in his breast; let the cough shake him. What of it? For four weeks he has been lying in bed, and what has it helped? No, it is absolutely his obligation to represent the Burial Society and to see to it that all is done ritually correct. By God, he is going to be there, even if he has to walk on crutches.

People were shocked when the old man who was known to be seriously ill appeared unexpectedly. Ghostly pale, he upset the assembled with his rasping cough and wheezing so that they advised him not to risk his health out of a false sense of duty, but to go home immediately. They were motivated not only by compassion but also by the desire to get rid of his disturbing presence. In vain. Stubborn as always, he insisted on staying. He even declined to ride in one of the numerous carriages. Instead he put himself at the head of the procession to lead it on foot. Everything seemed to take its orderly course when, just a few minutes before reaching the cemetery, Trendel suffered a hemorrhage and collapsed. He was transported home under the care of a doctor, but there was some grumbling complaint that the solemnity had been upset by Trendel's unreasonableness.

Now he was again laid up in his apartment. The nurse, that the congregation had provided, he had dismissed as soon as he felt somewhat improved. A widower, he had no close relations in town. Only the companions of the *Chevra Kaddishah* called with some regularity, and recently there appeared almost daily a female visitor: little Ruth. Although her father had not shown up at Trendel's ever since his offer to help had been rejected so rudely, he had commended him to his wife's care and insisted that Ruth should occasionally be sent up to him on errands. For educational reasons, Mr. Walter thought it useful that the child should get some insight into the looks of poverty.

Initially the little one had not been too enthusiastic about these missions, especially since the morose oldster had not been overly friendly and accepted what she brought as routinely as a deity its sacrifice. But that had changed gradually. It seemed that as he grew progressively weaker, Trendel felt guilty toward the child for his earlier death prophecies. Perhaps it occurred to him in the many lonesome hours, during which he had become increasingly anxious about his sickness, that someone among those people who walked around out there in such provocative good health might have already prognosed his death the way he once had done. Repentant, he tried to reconcile fate by changing his attitude and rewarding the trouble the child took with him with greater friendliness. Since he did not quite know what to talk to her about and how to entertain her, he just encouraged her to sample the sweets and fruit that visitors had brought and to sit a while at his bedside. Ruth was quick in noticing the change in his behavior and lost her uneasiness and shyness. She thought she knew from experience what patients enjoy and tried to amuse him in her own way. She chatted of this and that, without worrying much if it could interest him. So she would relate some school prank, a story or even an old fairy tale. Trendel let her be. Since speaking was hard on him and caused new painful coughing spells, he was content to listen and to prove his attention by throwing in an occasional remark. Sometimes, though, he fell asleep in spite of the girl's high, lively voice. Ruth got scared every time that happened. Terribly frightened, she bent over him to check if the cover on his breast still moved up and down and relaxed only when she could hear the faint sound of his breath.

One afternoon when Ruth was sitting at her patient's bedside, she brought up, with the lack of tact that seems to be the privilege of children, the tale of Godfather Death. She and her classmates intended to offer the story as a school play, and so she felt it necessary to provide a detailed account of it. Patiently, Trendel listened as she told the sinister fable. How Death is chosen Godfather to a poor boy. How he makes his godson a rich and famous physician by showing him a wonder-drug herb that can cure even the hopelessly ill. How the miracle works only when Godfather Death appears at the head of the patient's bed. How the young doctor tries to cheat Death out of his booty by turning the sick around when he sees his godfather standing at the foot of the bed.

Normally Trendel would have followed the story with fascinated interest and might have enriched it with some realistic contributions from his wide professional experience. But his relationship to death was changed now that he himself had felt the icy breath of the Inexorable. He, whose lifeblood–strange to say–had been death, who had met death so often that he seemed to have divested it of its terrifying mystery, he had begun to mistrust his patron, full of anxiety. He still joined in when his *Chevra* brethren talked shop, but it was bare routine. Left alone, the fear of death tortured him constantly. He felt he had to be on guard in order not to be taken by surprise by the Terrible One. No wonder then, that what impressed him most in Ruth's story was the ruse with which the doctor had outwitted Godfather Death. Following a sudden inspiration, he interrupted Ruth and asked if she would dare to contact the professor who had made her well so that he would come to see him. But by no means should she mention anything about that to her father. More and more urgent he got in his request. He told her in detail how to go about it and what to say to the doctor. He took her hand and forced her to swear that she would act exactly as instructed. Then he ordered her to go immediately.

Ruth returned home, equally confused and anguished by the inexplicable and almost threatening excitement of the old man as by the injunction not to talk to her father, without whose permission she did not dare to act. The mother noticed the child's unusual behavior and, concerned, asked for its reason. At first, Ruth would not talk; but in the evening when Mrs. Walter came to the girl's bedroom for a good-night kiss and again tried to persuade her to disclose what was troubling her, she broke into tears and disconsolately sobbing told what had happened up there at Mr. Trendel's and what she had to promise him. In the end, she begged never again to be sent up to Mr. Trendel. Mrs. Walter calmed the excited child and without delay sent word to her husband, who the same evening requested Professor Silberberg to take over Trendel's treatment.

The professor was prompt in coming. Radiating light and confidence as always, he entered the room of the sick man. But Trendel was very subdued.

"You probably are surprised, Professor," he began hesitatingly, "that someone like me should send for you. Actually I have no right to ask for the services of an authority like you and nobody has to know about it. On the other hand, everybody has some savings and if you could be a bit accommmodating . . . " He tried to smile, "After all my life is at stake."

Professor Silberberg, who had been briefed by Mr. Walter for the eventuality of the money question coming up, waved off Trendel's apprehension.

"Come, Mr. Trendel, aren't you ashamed of yourself? You know I am not that hungry. Sure, I have to live too, but that does not mean that I can not afford to treat somebody for nothing once in a while. First of all, let us see now what is wrong with you." And he began the examination.

It took long and was very thorough. Trendel followed every motion of the doctor with tense attention. When he listened to the heart, the old man stared fixedly at the face above him. Standing in judgment before the authority that would mete out life or death, trembling in fear and hope, he wished to tear out the thought from behind his judge's forehead. But that was steeled against this type of attack and remained impenetrable. Exhausted by the examination, Trendel abandoned the attempt to guess what was in store for him. In weak resignation, he waited for a decisive pronouncement. Professor Silberberg straightened up and looked at the patient in a kind of summing-up manner, as if he wanted to verify the findings inside the body by its outside aspect. Then, without saying anything definite about the result of the examination, he simply gave some instructions, chatted a little longer and turned to leave.

When he extended his hand to say goodbye, Trendel grabbed it in mortal fear. Everything in him rebelled against the doctor's taciturnity. He wanted certainty. How was it with him? Death or life? That was what counted. At the same time, he was terribly afraid to know the truth. Fear shook him. With great effort, he brought out hoarsely the hope-begging question.

"It isn't anything really dangerous, is it, Professor?"

Even Silberberg, in spite of all his self-control, shuddered, confronted with the desperate man's hunger for life. His answer, a painfully carefree, "Of course not!" was poorly acted. Once more he pressed the old man's hand and took a hurried departure. To Attorney Walter who was waiting for him he disclosed the hopelessness of the case.

And Trendel? . . . Hoped. Yes, he, Siegfried Trendel, who knew death better than many know life, who could recall only once being wrong about the outcome of an illness, he was willing to be deceived a second time, although the doctor's evasive lie was so obvious. "Of course not" had been the answer to his anxious question. He clung to those miserable few words and tried to detect in them the reassurance which in truth had been absent.

All that is left now to say is a word about Trendel's funeral. It was as honorable as was fitting for the most active member of the *Chevra Kaddishah*. The most distinguished of his pious companions stood around his coffin and carried him to the grave. The rabbi eulogized him beautifully as a true man of God and found the right words to fill the numerous assembly with respect for the service that Siegfried Trendel had rendered to the community for so many years. The congregants were genuinely touched and felt bad for the lack of appreciation of which many knew themselves guilty. Unfortunately people often get ashamed of sincere repentant feelings and hasten to hide a rising tear under a forced frivolity. So when the mourning crowd disbanded, the remark was heard that it was a shame that Trendel could not have witnessed the *Koved* (honors) at his funeral with his own eyes, and somebody found it necessary to express jokingly his satisfaction that finally the old *Neshome-Khopper*'s turn had come.

CHANGE OF MIND

Enough of bombings, knifings, rapings,
Of drug-sicks that on sidewalks roam,
Enough of hospitals and chest pain.
    I want to go home.
    I want to go home.

A sunray redding the horizon,
A bubbling coffeepot, a dog's wet nose,
A turning lock. She standing in the doorway,
    I change my mind.
    I want to stay.
    I want to stay.

Typesetting
The Type Shop, Durham, NC

Cover Illustration
Martell Design, Durham, NC

Printing
Watermark Graphics, Apex, NC